The Pardoner's Tale

Morgan Ferdinand

Copyright © 2014 Morgan Ferdinand

All rights reserved.

ISBN: 1500874485
ISBN-13: 978-1500874483

DEDICATION

For mom and Ian and assorted cats.

ACKNOWLEDGMENTS

The Pardoner's Tale and *Ace of Wands* were originally published as ebooks by Torquere Press. I'm grateful to them for publishing me, getting me started, and sending me royalty checks until the contracts ran out. This book combines the two stories published by Torquere Press and some additional short stories. There have been some modifications made to the previously published text.

Table of Contents

Book One: The Pardoner's Tale 5

Book Two: Ace of Wands 137

Short Stories 183

Morgan Ferdinand

Book One: The Pardoner's Tale

Morgan Ferdinand

Chapter One

The sign on the heavy oak door said Nicholas Pardoner, Private Investigator. The nameplate on the desk also read Nicholas Pardoner. The man seated in the battered leather chair, feet propped up on the desk, baseball cap over his eyes to block out the fluorescent lights, arms folded across his chest, and shirtsleeves rolled up, was the so-named Nicholas Pardoner, private investigator.

In other words, that was me. It was a Tuesday at ten in the morning and I'd already grown tired of repeated games of solitaire. I had a sticky-note on my monitor reminding me to download new games after my nap. Also on the desk (beside my computer and my feet) there was a cup of coffee gone cold, a very silent telephone, and a mobile phone that also served as a mobile computer (also in need of new games).

I'd really like to say something along the lines of the dame appeared before me, looking scared. Her blue eyes were wide with fear and her hands trembled as she shook my hand. "Mister Pardoner," she said, "I need you to find my father, Professor Smith. He's been kidnapped and I think they're coming for me next." I'd love to say that. That would be completely awesome. That would be the sort of thing that led me to become a detective in the first place.

But I'd be lying if I said that, because what actually happened was that two young men with very white smiles and neatly pressed suits knocked on my door and asked me if I'd found God. I told them I hadn't, but I could for two hundred a day plus expenses. They weren't amused and left just as quickly as they'd arrived.

I settled back in my chair to resume my nap.

Later that night I went to my favorite bar. There's nothing better, after a long day spent doing nothing except paying bills and watching the bank account dwindle, than a trip to the bar and a whole lot of alcohol.

There was nothing special about the place. It was just a standard dive bar. Popular with the locals, and not much of a draw for the tourists. That was why a stranger walking in caught my attention. That was what caught everyone's attention initially, but the man was given the onceover by the regulars, who then turned back to their drinks or their conversations or their games.

I didn't look away. I watched him carefully, keeping my head down just enough not to draw his attention, but my eyes raised so that I could track his progress through the bar. He sat down on a bar stool, not too near the window, but near enough that he could watch people on the street as they hurried past in the fading daylight. He ordered a draft beer. It wasn't anything fancy or expensive, but something told me his usual tastes were more exotic than Coors Light.

Dark hair, cut short in a very common, tidy style. Strong nose, sharp chin highlighted by five o'clock shadow. He was dressed conservatively in jeans and a black T-shirt and looked like any other blue-collar worker stopping off for a beer on his way home. If anyone else but me looked at him, that's exactly what they would have believed him to be.

However, this man had the unfortunate luck of stepping into the bar I call home on a night I was there. Another day or even a few hours later and I wouldn't have been there. He could have come and gone without my knowing a thing about it.

Maybe it was just his bad luck. Maybe it was just my good luck. I didn't really care. I touched the handgun in my jacket pocket and smiled behind the edge of my glass. I tossed thirty dollars next to my collection of glasses and signaled the waitress. Thirty would cover my tab and leave a very generous tip.

Once I started walking I realized I might have had a few too many. I ducked into an alley to wait for my victim and leaned against the wall for support.

It was an hour before he left the bar. I noticed he had a slight limp. A little hitch in his left leg. It didn't seem to hurt him or slow him down, but the potential weakness was valuable information.

There was a split second of time when I could have grabbed him and dragged him into the alley.

I know you're thinking, "You had a gun. Why not just pop him right there and get the hell out?" The gun was my last resort. The gun was only there to make sure that he was well and truly dead, after I had done what I needed to do.

It should have been easy. Grab him, drag him back, slit his throat, and then remove his heart.

Shoot him in the head. Watch the body turn to dust. Basic vampire extermination one-oh-one.

What they don't tell you is that when hiding in alleys you've got to remember to adjust for garbage. I stepped on a wet, waxy, fast food wrapper that was lying in a slick of rancid oil. Instead of dragging my target back into the alley I fell on top of him, pinning him to the sidewalk. We were out in the open on a busy Tuesday night, with tourists and college students walking past and staring.

The target grabbed my throat and threw me off him and into the alley. I hit the wall and bounced into the trash bags stacked up next to the back door of a restaurant. Raw fish parts and rotting vegetables oozed out.

He was barely breathing hard when he grabbed me by the shoulders and hauled me to my feet. It was no effort for him to lift me and pin me against the wall. His eyes flashed black and he snarled, revealing distended canines. "Fuck you," he growled and thrust me hard against the wall. The back of my head connected with the bricks and for a moment everything went dark grey and fuzzy. I shook my head and things slipped back into focus.

That seemed to surprise him. His nostrils flared as he studied me and his lips parted slightly. He was tasting as well as smelling the air between us. I wondered how he felt about rotting fish guts.

"You're not like the others," he said finally. He seemed uncertain of what he was looking at. I stretched, desperately trying to get my feet on the ground. Being held up like that was starting to make breathing difficult. I made a soft gagging sound when I tried to speak.

He lowered me so my toes could touch the ground, but he kept a solid grip on my shoulders. I couldn't go left, right, and when he planted one foot between mine so his knee and hip were pressed against my groin I couldn't go down. "What are you?"

"Shifter. Can't you smell it?"

He leaned in close, his nose almost touching mine. "Right now the only thing I can smell is garbage and beer. Prove it."

"I'm not going to prove it to you!"

"Why not?"

"In the middle of an alley?"

"You were going to kill me in the middle of an alley!"

"That's different!"

"How do you figure?"

"You'd turn to dust and there'd be no body or evidence that it had happened."

"Witnesses?"

"Drunks and whores."

"Ah-hah! You just cut your own throat with that." He glanced at the knife on the ground. "Metaphorically speaking."

He had me there. Literally speaking.

"It's not the full moon."

"I'll be damned," the vampire replied. Then everything went black.

I woke up three hours later. I was still in the alley, but I was alone. I had no idea where the vampire had gone, and why he had stolen my wallet and my knife, or why he'd left me the gun. I had a headache, a mouth that tasted of old socks, and a sick feeling in my stomach. As far as I could tell I hadn't been bitten or harmed in any way. Why hadn't he just killed me when I was clearly going to kill him?

The sun was up by the time I got home. I knew it'd be pointless to go hunting for the vampire, since I had no idea where he might be hiding. There'd been no reports of activity. I hadn't even known there was one in the area. I just knew that I had a standing contract to eliminate all vampires, no questions asked.

It took me three showers to get the garbage smell off my skin. I checked myself several times, looking to see if there was any indication that I'd been bitten. My clothes were dirty, but there was no blood anywhere and no marks on me. Then I settled myself in front of the computer, checked my email, checked my sources, and found nothing. No mention of a vampire. Either he was very new in town or very good at his job. I was opting for new in town, although I had enough bruises and scrapes telling me he might just be that good.

I knew this would be a tough job. I was looking forward to the challenge. I slept until the sun went down, then I packed my things and went hunting. Unfortunately, my efforts were completely unproductive. There wasn't a trace of him anywhere. Not a sign of feeding, not a sighting, not a whisper of activity the whole night. It was possible that he'd been transient. That his happening into my bar was just a one-off for him, and he was out of my territory as quickly as he'd arrived.

Until I got home. The vampire was sitting on my front steps. So much for my challenge.

He flicked ashes from the end of his cigarette and squinted at me. "What the fuck was all that about?"

"I was just doing my job."

"Your job is dusting me, or all of us?"

"All of you. Nothing personal, so — no offense."

"Oh, none taken!" His upper lip curled in a snarl and I braced myself for an attack that didn't come. I opened one eye and looked at him. He ground his cigarette out against the step and shrugged. "Just doing your job, right? Dust the vampires and rid the world of the scourge. What do you get out of it? The curse lifted?"

I sat down next to him and stole a cigarette from his pack. He handed me a lighter. "Nah. Like I said. It's just a job. I was born this way so it's not something that can be removed like that." I snapped my fingers.

"No kidding? I was turned when I was in college. Drunk at a party, took the wrong person home."

"I didn't ask for your life story." I handed him back the lighter and exhaled smoke into his face.

"How come I'm not killing you right now?"

"You're intrigued by my story, my charm, and my youthful good looks."

"And shocked by your modesty." I pinched the bridge of my nose between my thumb and index finger and rubbed the base of my skull with the other hand. It had been a long night. Fortunately, being self-employed meant there wasn't anyone to yell at me for taking two days off without warning. I was going to need a very long nap after this encounter.

"So why do you do this? As a career, I mean."

"Well, I don't. Not really. I'm a private investigator. The vampire-killing is sort of a sideline. A sub-contract job, you could say." I leaned back against the door, chatting calmly while at the same time a tiny voice in the back of my mind was demanding to know what I was doing. "Kill him, you fucker!" It screamed at me. "You get paid to terminate vampires and you're sitting there having a little chat with one!" I shut the voice into an imaginary box and glanced sideways at the vampire as he stubbed out a second cigarette against my steps. "Stop doing that."

"Haven't got an ashtray." He flicked the butt into the gutter.

I sighed and stood, fishing my keys from my pocket. "Come on, then. The sun'll be up soon, anyhow. You're invited blah blah blah."

The vampire stood up, brushed off the seat of his pants, and followed me in. He stood in the middle of the living room, looking around as if slightly amazed by all the bookshelves lining the walls. Most of them were packed with books. Several of them held cardboard boxes of various sizes. Some of the shelves were covered in stone carvings of various gods and wolves, other sorts of tribal decoration, and a few random toys from local fast food chains.

"Eclectic. I like it. How old are you?"

I locked up my weapons (keeping a stake handy, just in case) and looked up at his question.

"Thirty-four. Why?"

He trailed his fingers along the curve of a goddess figure. "I think I was just wondering if you were, you know, there when these things were made."

"We don't work like you lot. We age just like everyone else. Well, maybe a little faster actually.

Shifting takes a lot out of a body."

"You lied to me."

"I did?"

"Last night when you said you couldn't shift because it wasn't a full moon."

"It wasn't a full moon."

"Either you lied about not being able to shift or you lied about being born a were. Born were aren't bound by the phases of the moon."

"I lied about not being able to shift. How'd you know that, anyhow?"

The vampire shrugged one shoulder. "I read. Mind if I have a seat?"

"What's your name?"

"Vlad." He grinned and winked.

I raised my clenched hands, prepared to fight. "Funny. Now what's your real name?"

"Alex. What's yours?" He made it a challenge.

"Van Helsing."

"Liar!" He jabbed a finger at me. "What sort of friendship will this be if I can't trust you?"

"Friendship?" I shouted, squeaking a little with surprise. "I'm supposed to kill you! You drugged me! And you lied about your name!"

He sniffed and studied his nails. "I was evening the score. Now you're a lie ahead of me."

I stammered. I huffed. The vampire folded his arms across his chest and fixed me with a gaze that made me feel like I'd been caught doing something wrong. "How old are you?"

"Thirty-two," he said.

"Liar! We're even now."

"Fact! I was born at eleven fifty-nine on the twenty-fourth of December, nineteen seventy-three. My name is Alexander Dwight Finch, and I'm a Capricorn. I like long walks in the moonlight and the taste of blood. Look, can I have a seat or not?" He stared at me. "Your little 'blah blah blah' was okay to let me come in, but I'm sort of... uninvited for everything else."

"Welcome to my home, Alex Finch. Please feel free to sit or use the bathroom or the kitchen. Don't touch anything on the shelves and stay out of my bedroom." The pain in my neck was slowly creeping up to the top of my skull.

"That's not fair! You could come out here and kill me in my sleep, but I don't get the same opportunity?"

"House rules." I turned to the stairs, ready to head for a shower and then to bed. "Name's Nicholas, by the way. Good night."

"Good morning!" he called with mocking cheerfulness.

***

Several hours later, I found him sitting on the foot of my bed. "Now we're even. I lied about the invitation thing. Here's your wallet. I kept the cash. Good night."

I caught the wallet when he flipped it to me and I watched him leave the room. I didn't go back to sleep the rest of the day. At sunset, I found him in the kitchen, frying a large quantity of bacon. He looked fit. Content. Well rested. I caught a glimpse of myself reflected in the shiny black surface of the refrigerator. I was none of these things.

"You look like hell, Nicky." He assembled a bacon sandwich (with mayo on toasted rye) and took a healthy bite.

"Nicholas," I growled, torn between irritation and something like relief that he'd also made coffee.

The vampire leaned over the stove and lit a cigarette at one of the burners. I had a brief flash of grabbing the back of his head and slamming it into the flames. He offered the cigarette to me. "Sandwich?" He said as I took a drag.

I thought about it for a few seconds while I exhaled. "Yeah, all right. You know I kill vampires, right?"

"I'm aware."

"No, I'm a were. You're a vampire."

"You're not so good with comedy, Nicky."

"Nicholas. One day I'm going to stake you."

"No you won't," he said as he handed me a mug of coffee.

"Why not?" I rubbed the back of my neck, trying to massage out the kinks of not sleeping.

"I make amazing coffee."

I took a sip. He was right. His sandwich wasn't bad, either.

***

Over the next few days, Alex moved into my home, made use of my kitchen, and picked up this annoying habit of moving my things around, but he stayed out of my bedroom, which was a small comfort. Each day I asked him why I hadn't killed him yet. Each day he offered me a crooked grin and a coffee instead of a reason. Maybe that was reason enough.

Chapter Two

Two weeks later, we were at the bar - that bar, the bar where it all began. We sat at a table near the back, where I could see the door and the window. It might have been the same table I was sitting at the first time I saw Alex. We sat in silence. I listened to the conversations around me. Alex watched the television mounted over the bar. It was a quiet evening and I was just starting to enjoy myself.

Naturally, that meant my cell phone had to vibrate.

I read the text message, stood up, and stretched. I fished some money from my wallet and handed it to Alex. "Find your own way home, pal. I've got to go to work."

"We."

"You speaking French or implying that you're coming with me?"

"I'm coming with you."

"Okay." I nodded once. "Why?"

He gave me his one-shoulder shrug. "Keep your friends close and your enemies closer?"

I sighed and shrugged in return. I didn't see any harm in taking him with me. It wasn't anything dangerous or even interesting that I was being summoned to do. See, I'm not just a private investigator and I don't just hunt vampires. Mostly what I did was collection of possessed antiques and artifacts with the occasional exorcism thrown in. I went over the details of my job while we returned home.

"You're a retriever," Alex said flatly when I explained what I did. The struggle to contain his laughter was valiant, but in vain. He threw himself into the chair he had claimed as his own and laughed until he was breathless.

"It's not that funny, Alex."

"You don't have the image I have. You, with a big fluffy tail, trotting down the street with the handle of a vase in your teeth."

"Why would I be shifted?"

"You weren't. I just threw in the tail because it was funny."

I lovingly caressed the stake that I kept near the couch. He shut up.

Alex watched me tap away at the computer. "So tell me what we're looking for?"

"It's not what as much as it is who. What do you know about schizophrenia?" I jotted notes and continued to type and click. Alex curled up in the seat of the chair, dangling his legs over the arm. He lit a cigarette and exhaled slowly, watching the light get caught in the smoke as it drifted toward the ceiling.

"Hallucinations. Delusions. Makes me think of crazy people on the street, shuffling around talking to Elvis or Jesus or aliens."

"That's it. But sometimes it's not just all in their heads. Sometimes it's somewhere else inside them."

"What's that mean? That they really are talking to Elvis?"

"Elvis or maybe some demon that likes to call itself Elvis. Or might actually be named Elvis. I've never really gotten too personal with them."

Alex swung his legs to the front of the chair and leaned forward, staring at me. "I just find it a little hard to believe that there are demons hanging out in people who don't have anything better to do than make them shuffle around and beg for spare change. I mean, shouldn't it be more like spreading evil and hate and converting people to the side of darkness or something?"

"That is what I'm telling you." I jotted down an address and shut down the computer. I looked at him. His mouth was set in a straight line and one eyebrow was cocked in clear disbelief. "It's funny that you of all people don't believe me. Think about it. You see those people and you get angry, don't you? Wish they'd just die or go away. You don't want them touching you. You don't want them talking to you. You look away. Ignore them. Cross the street to get away from them. Not very nice, right? Add up a whole bunch of little sins all the time and you end up with one very bad soul."

I stood up and shoved Alex back in his chair so I could walk past him. I picked up my jacket and the black leather backpack that held the essential tools for my job. Without even bothering to wait for Alex, I left the house. I wasn't in the mood for a theological debate.

Alex caught up with me at the car. He slid into the passenger seat and buckled the seatbelt while I sat there staring at the dash, my forehead resting on the steering wheel. Alex nudged my shoulder. "You believe in demons, but you don't believe in God, do you." It wasn't a question.

"If God existed, then I would be normal." I put the car in reverse and slid out of the parking space.

"I think you're pretty normal. All things considered, I mean. I don't know any other were, so I don't know if you're normal compared to them. But as far as people go, you seem just fine to me. A little bit weird about your CD collection…."

I growled.

Alex propped his elbow on the door and leaned against his hand. "Anyhow, you're okay."

***

The subject was a man in his early seventies. His daughter had reported him missing when she went to his house to bring him groceries. She had assumed his strange behavior was just part of getting old—that his talking to himself and his forgetfulness and occasional violent outbursts were just the start of Alzheimer's disease—and she'd made up her mind that day to talk to him about going to see a doctor. Instead she'd found herself sitting in the police station, giving his description to an officer.

The woman was tearful, babbling about things that the officer really wasn't concerned with. He just needed a recent photo, a list of people who might have seen him, and places where the old man liked to go. One of the clerks, however, was interested to hear how he'd been doing so well on his own and how proud he was that he could take care of himself. Then a month ago, after they'd been to a flea market, he'd suddenly taken a downturn.

The clerk (Linda) brought the woman a cup of terrible coffee and whispered to the officer that she would talk to the woman a little and help her calm down. The officer, glad to have someone take the nearly hysterical woman off his hands, said that would be just fine with him. The clerk asked about the flea market. She was an avid flea market shopper she said. What had he bought? The woman thought about it and said that the last thing she remembered him buying was a porcelain dog figurine. She thought it was ugly, but he seemed pleased with it. It wasn't going to be in her house, so she couldn't really complain.

Then, three days later when she stopped by to drop off some books for him, he'd suddenly gotten old and forgetful. She started visiting him every day after that, to make sure he was eating and bathing and using the bathroom.

The clerk stopped listening after the part about the figurines, but sat with the woman anyhow, nodding and saying "I see" and "poor dear" in all the right places. Once the woman was calm the clerk sent her back to the officer and then she sent the emails that started the process.

The text message informing me of a task was the next to last link in the chain. Details were in my email, and after a little checking of on-line maps, I was ready to go.

Alex fiddled with the radio while I drove. Occasionally he read me directions, complaining about my handwriting. We found our first location and I checked my watch.

"I shouldn't have let you come with me."

"Why not?"

"It's sunrise in about fifteen minutes." I pointed east. "See that?"

Alex nodded slowly. "I suppose now would be a good time to tell you that I'm not bothered by sunlight, huh?"

I lit a cigarette and handed it to him after the first drag. "How does that work?"

"No idea, man." He turned to face me and grinned. "You're supposed to be the expert. Or are you keeping me around for research purposes?"

"I could kill you and send you off for research."

"You'd have to go back to making your own coffee."

Vampire, one. Werewolf, zero.

"Do you come from a family of shifters?"

"I'm the only one in my family. I've been living on my own since I was seventeen because it started to get too difficult to hide what was going on."

"Teen Wolf." Alex said. "You ever see that movie?"

"I Was a Teenage Werewolf, you mean?"

"The one with that guy from television."

"Yeah, Michael Landon."

"No, the other one. The one in the eighties."

"I think we can safely assume I haven't seen it."

"You don't watch werewolf movies, do you."

"Do you watch vampire films?"

"Well, yeah! They're fun! And they're informative. I don't think I would have lived this long if I didn't have some idea of what was going on and what to do. Everything I learned, I learned from the movies. I mean, there's not exactly anyone around who teaches these things. You can't just look up 'Vampire' in the yellow pages and find a teacher. So if you don't watch werewolf movies how did you work things out?"

"I just made it up as I went alo—" I trailed off as I became aware of the subject making his way down the street, walking directly toward the car. I could smell the demon inside him. "Alex. Can you, like, enchant people?"
"Like, what do you mean?"

"Like, calm them. Make them more receptive to something. I mean, what do you do when you're about to feed off someone? You must do something to put them at ease, right?"

"Yeah, I can do that. Why?"

"Have you ever ripped a demon out of someone's body?"

"No, but I can imagine it'd be unpleasant."

"Exactly. I need you to make sure that man there doesn't freak out and cause a scene."

Alex licked his lips and nodded. "Easy. Calm him down, you do what you need to do, and then we're out of there."

"That's it exactly. C'mon." I patted his shoulder and got out of the car. I went through the motions of looking around at the addresses on buildings while Alex walked toward the subject. The subject jerked away and started babbling. It wasn't English and I'm not fluent in demon, but judging by the way he was reacting to Alex, the demon had a pretty good idea that Alex wasn't your average guy. This was not going nice and smooth like I'd hoped it would. I felt the hair on my arms and the nape of my neck stand up and wrote it off as adrenaline.

Alex put his right hand on the man's chest. The man grew quiet almost instantly and stared at

Alex with a look of pain and fear. Alex was pale. "Nicky, hurry. I can't hold this for too long."

I rushed over to the two of them and we lowered the subject to the ground. Alex backed away to give me room to work. "If I call for an ambulance, how long do you think it'd take them to get here?"

"Five, maybe ten minutes. I'm not sure. Why?"

"Because I stopped his heart. I don't want him to suffer from that. How long will this take you?"

I had already begun the process of finding the demon. I had a small, iron ball pressed against the man's sternum and was just about to begin the chant that would draw the demon out and into the ball. I stopped and looked at Alex. "You did what?"

"It's okay. I can start it again. It's just that he's old and not in the best health. I'd like to call the paramedics and get them here as fast as possible."

I tossed my mobile phone to him. "Back up to make the call. I don't want the phone interfering and I don't want you distracting me." Alex made the call and I performed the ritual. The demon was pulled from the man's body and trapped inside the hollow iron ball.

The pellet shook and rolled in my hand as we stood over the man. The paramedics arrived. The man's daughter arrived. The police arrived. After several cups of coffee from a nearby carryout and repeated statement to the police and medical staff it was determined that he was really lucky that we happened to be in the area when he suffered a heart attack, and that Alex's phone call to emergency services saved his life.

The man's daughter was grateful. She threw her arms around Alex's neck and kissed him repeatedly. I stood away from them, hands stuffed in my pockets, protecting the iron ball.

It was nearly mid-day when we arrived at home. I was starving. Alex was dead on his feet. So to speak. He passed out on the couch while I made a sandwich and took it to my room.

I tossed the iron ball with the demon inside into a jar on my dresser. It held about thirty balls of various sizes. All of them trembled and vibrated with the buzz of tiny, captive demons. The clicking and buzzing lulled me to sleep.

The next morning, I went to my office to sit around and wait for nothing to happen. The first thing I did was check my bank account. The payment for the exorcism had been deposited. I transferred most of it to my savings account and paid a few bills. Even werewolves need to make sure the utilities are taken care of.

I turned to research next. Part of my job requires keeping up with the news, sorting out what might be a demon or a vampire or some other occurrence that couldn't be easily attributed to anything "natural" (I refuse to consider myself "supernatural" or "unnatural". I was born this way, so what could be more natural than that?).

After three hours online and countless websites visited I learned that there were at least six demons at work over in the Dayton area that I'd need to contend with. I found three with little problem. They were clustered together in an abandoned building. I rounded them up and contained them in about two hours.

Technically, they were poltergeists. They'd taken to throwing bricks at people and cars. The police were certain it was some sort of gang initiation and had been frustrated by repeated attempts to get information from the locals. No one ever saw anyone going in or out of the building, except for the occasional homeless person, and most of them barely had the strength to stand, let alone throw bricks through windshields.

The others were going to take a little more searching. They didn't seem to be tied to a location, or were tied to something portable. This would take some tracking. I reported the capture of the three poltergeists, did a little more research, and called it a day.

My research reinforced one very important thing I knew about vampires: most of the information about them is crap. Most people writing about vampires—writing "nonfiction" about vampires—

are insane. The discourses on "psychic vampires" and "emotional vampires" and why and how people become vampires were faulty at best and dangerous at its worst. The people claiming to *be* vampires would probably drop dead of a heart attack if they ever encountered an actual vampire.

Well. Maybe not any vampire. The unmistakable sound of Madness greeted me when I opened my front door and I found

Alex ska dancing in the living room.

I sighed and sat down on the sofa. It was good having Alex around. I was starting to enjoy having him around. He didn't mind taking care of things around the house. He was someone I could talk to about things my neighbors wouldn't understand. I didn't have to hide what I was from him. He was in no position to judge me, and his strength meant there was someone around who was capable of controlling me if I ever got carried away in a shift. I was starting to consider this vampire a friend, so maybe I should lighten up a little.

"And what vampire movies do you suggest?" I asked, grudgingly.

Alex and I spent nearly ten hours watching movies, interrupted only long enough to use the bathroom and answer the door to accept deliveries of pizza and Chinese. At the end of it I was tired and confused. Alex was bloated and sleepy.

"I'm no better off than I was before." I yawned and picked a Lo Mein noodle from my shirt.

"Let me get this straight. You hunt vampires. You kill them. But you know nothing about them?" He hiccupped.

"It's not like there was a qualifying exam! Anyhow, you defy the rules that I thought I knew. I've watched you put away food covered in garlic. You're not at all bothered by sunlight. The whole running water thing doesn't stop you from taking an hour long shower. For all I know, you could be a practicing Catholic."

"Lapsed, actually."

"See!" I stood and threw my hands up in frustration.

"Everything I knew is wrong, and all these stupid movies did nothing but give me conflicting information!"

Alex shrugged and shook his head. "Fun to watch, though. I hadn't seen a couple of those in years."

"Alex."

"Nicholas."

"Are you actually a vampire or are you just some sort of homeless lunatic?"

He opened and closed his mouth so many times he looked like a goldfish. Then he lunged.

Enough time had passed since our rumble in the alley that I'd forgotten he had a serious amount of strength packed into his unassuming frame. I often forgot he was a vampire at all. I had put myself in a very dangerous position.

Alex was behind me, arms wrapped around my head. It would only take a small gesture for him to snap my neck. His breath was hot against my ear. "If I weren't a vampire, I wouldn't be able to calm people down for you. If I weren't a vampire you never would have *noticed* me. We wouldn't be having this little dance right now." His teeth grazed my neck, and then he pushed me away with enough force to send me into the wall. I clamped my hand to the spot where I'd felt his teeth; there was no blood. Not even a welt.

"That was just a warning, you big baby." He was angry.

"Go feed," I growled. "Go find yourself a victim." I pulled out my wallet and handed him cash. "Have a whore. My treat!" Hey, I was angry too.

Alex grabbed the cash, flipped me a salute, and left.

He returned just before sunrise. He stood in the doorway to my bedroom, staring at me until I woke up.

I sat up and switched on the light next to the bed. "Did you want something?"

He threw the money back at me. "So you know, I didn't kill anyone tonight. I didn't even feed."

What did he want me to do, congratulate him? I collected the scattered bills, stacked them neatly on the bedside table and turned the light off. "Goodnight, Alex."

"Good morning, Nicky." He slammed the door behind him.

I looked at the door. I got out of bed and pulled clothes on. I stalked my way to the living room.

Alex was sprawled across the couch with headphones on.

I kicked his foot. "Show me."

He slipped the headphones off one ear. "Show you what?"

"Do something vampiric. Give me a reason to kill you. Do something to prove to me you are a vampire, so I can justify killing you."

"I asked you first. That night in the alley. I wanted proof you were a shifter, remember? I've still never seen you shift."

"I'll show you mine if you show me yours." I quipped.

He stood up and moved close. We were (almost) eye-to-eye. Had his eyes always been that oddly dark shade of blue? I was aware of his breath hitting my face in angry little puffs. It was fresh with the scent of mouthwash. His skin smelled of the soap in the bathroom. There was an underlying salty smell to him and it reminded me of the ocean. This close I could see the very faint start of stubble on his cheeks and chin. Wildly, I wondered if his face would feel rough if I touched it. I raised my hand and lightly brushed my fingertips across his jaw, tilting my head to the left to watch the progress of my fingers. Everything seemed to be moving in slow motion. The hair at the nape of my neck rose.

He pressed the tip of his index finger against the vein in my throat. "Bang," he whispered, and suddenly the world returned to normal.

I backed away from him, blinking, and stuttering. "You asshole! What was that?"

The one-shoulder shrug. "You wanted proof. That's what it feels like when I'm about to feed. That's what makes it so easy. You get the idea that it'll be the most pleasurable thing you've ever experienced, so why should you stop me from doing it?"

"That's just fucking sick. You really do that to people?" I shivered and hugged myself.

He nodded and pressed his right hand against my chest. A dizzy feeling washed over me and breathing became difficult. I was getting lightheaded and I was aware that there was something was missing. My heartbeat.

Alex pulled his hand back and then shoved it hard against my chest. Not a punch, but a very hard shove. Suddenly everything came flooding back. I gasped and filled my lungs, clutching my chest to be certain my heart was actually beating.

"Your turn."

"I can't."

"You can. You're not bound by the moon."

"I mean I don't trust you. I'm not going to make myself vulnerable like that."

He raised one eyebrow. "I've already had countless opportunities to hurt or even kill you, you know. I'm faster, I'm stronger, and I do the cooking. I could drug your food or your fucking coffee and remove your heart or just feed from you while you were out cold. But if you'll notice I haven't done any of that. The worst thing I've done lately is let you drink milk that was just about to go off."

"You never did that."

"Well you smelled it first and threw it out, but I didn't stop you from opening it."

I hated it when he was right. It really pissed me off. "There's really no way I can get out of this, is there."

"Not really, no."

I turned around so my back was to Alex and briefly considered making a run for my room, but he could move faster and get there first and I hated having him in my bedroom. I pulled my T-shirt off.

"Whoa. Whoa! What are you doing?"

I looked back over my shoulder. "What? This is what I do. I can't shift when I'm dressed. Not unless I want to ruin what I'm wearing."

"For my sake? Ruin the jammies."

"Fuck off. You're just going to have to deal with seeing my bare butt for a few minutes." Pajama bottoms came down, were kicked to the side, and the process started.

The process was halted by a loud giggle.

I turned and looked back at him again. "What is your problem?"

"Nothing, man. That's just the hairiest ass I've seen in a while."

"Werewolf!" What did he expect? I don't have excess hair, really. It's just... darker and more obvious on me than it is on non-were. And maybe there is more of it. I've never been in a position to compare it to anyone else's.

He waved his hand dismissively. "Carry on."

Shifting is not an easy or comfortable process. It takes time and it usually requires somewhere that's soundproof. Have you ever broken a bone and had to have it re-broken so it could set properly? Try to imagine that happening to every bone in your body at once. Joints separate. Muscles stretch or contract. Your skin crawls as hair sprouts. Your teeth shift and your face stretches to accommodate your muzzle. The reshaping of your ears, the set of your eyes, your posture-- it all changes. Smells intensify. Sounds grow louder. Colors fade out. Top it off with suddenly obtaining a fluffy tail that insists on wagging itself and it's a humiliating, shocking transformation that you never quite get used to.

But I did it.

I made my way to my bedroom before reverting back to human form. I showered, letting abused muscle and bone relax under the hot spray. I'm always cold and sore after I shift, which is another reason I don't do it as often as I could.

***

The little display of skills broke the ice, and Alex and I worked as a team from that point on. In simple cases where I was just the courier, I trusted him to drive. If I was going to be "just a retriever", I might as well be a dignified one. It was nice to show up at an auction house or a consignment shop or even a pawn shop and have Alex wait in the car while I conducted business. Sometimes he was needed to help me carry something heavy or cumbersome, like the dresser with the poltergeist trapped in the one drawer that wouldn't open.

These were the best assignments. Very simple, no-one-gets-hurt affairs. Go somewhere, buy something, make the drop, and go home. By morning the cost of the purchase plus my fee was safely in my bank account. After each job I shuttled money into my savings account, made sure all the bills were paid (my rent was now paid for six months in advance), and then we'd go out to the bar or a restaurant or even a movie.

I really appreciated Alex's presence and his skills on the cases involving free-range demons. Things like exorcisms, or spirits that were attached-to but not locked inside items. Some of the smaller ones were afraid of Alex just because he was a vampire and it didn't matter that Alex was more afraid of them than they were of him. Demons don't expect vampires to be afraid of them so they don't look for the fear when they encounter one.

One particularly small demon who was really no threat at all (except he liked to hang out in vending machines and take people's money without giving them their purchase), voluntarily got into the iron ball, just so he'd be safely away from the "vicious vampire."

With bigger, more dangerous demons it was good to have someone stronger and faster than me. Once he pointed out that if we were being chased by something, he'd just have to outrun me. I replied that once it was through with me it'd be right back after him and demons don't get tired. Ever. The jar of wriggling, clicking, iron balls in my bedroom was proof of that.

"What will you do if you come up against a demon that isn't bound by iron?"

"Don't ask questions, Alex. Just drive."

"I was thinking about 'Ghostbusters' the other day."

"What's that?"

"Right. I forget that you don't watch movies. Never mind."

I watched the movie later. It doesn't work like that at all.

***

There are some benefits to being born a werewolf. I can shift when I want to or need to, regardless of the phase of the moon or the time of the day. The increased strength and speed are nice, but you have to actually work for them. You're not just born stronger. You've got to develop the muscles just like anyone else does. We've just got the ability to do more than your average, non-steroid-abusing human.

Seeing it written down, the perks of being a werewolf aren't really that impressive, since technology and medical science can give people a lot of what we shifters are born with. We're a genetic mutation and I think we're on the way out. The birth rate of shifter couples is low. Both shifters have to be the same animal to produce a child with the ability, and shifting is obviously recessive, so if only one parent carries the gene the odds of a child being a shifter are slim. Contrary to the myths, it's almost impossible for a shifter to pass on "the curse" to someone through an attack. I don't know if this is because most were don't need to attack anyone, or because very few people ever survive an attack when it does happen.

The down side of being a shifter is everything else. Increased sensitivity to light and sounds and smells, for one thing. You don't know what disgusting creatures humans are until you walk into a public restroom. Do that once and you'll never do it again if you can help it.

Until you get the hang of shifting and learn how to control it, it's worse than anything else that happens to so-called "normal" teenagers. While my friends were out discovering drugs and alcohol and their sexuality I was trying to figure out why I was – well, turning into a wolf. There isn't a school counselor around that can handle that sort of thing. Puberty makes most people grow hair in new places, but nothing like what I dealt with.

I finished high school at seventeen and moved out immediately into a small apartment near college. I couldn't handle the idea of a dorm and a communal bathroom. My unit was in the basement. I felt safe there. I told the landlord I was a musician and he let me install soundproofing. Better a little insulation than noise complaints and lost tenants, right? I was nineteen when I finally had enough control to not need to shift during a full moon.

I majored in law. I studied psychology, and photography. I took courses in crime scene forensics.

And through it all I worked for a collector who operated what he called a "dime museum." Albert Tyson encouraged me to take courses in archeology, history, anthropology, and he paid me more than enough for the simple job of rounding up his purchases.

I would drive all over the state of Ohio, and sometimes all over the mid-Atlantic region, picking up things that ranged from mundane and ugly to downright creepy. Old dental equipment. Things that looked like torture devices. Obviously fake "oddities" like the two-headed cat with very visible stitching holding the second head in place. And some things looked completely benign but touching them made me feel uncomfortable. Almost violated.

After graduation, I worked full time for him, expanding my retrievals to all parts of the continental United States. Eventually he confronted me. Asked me what I was. What I *really* was. He stressed it in a way that let me know there wasn't a point to lying. I'd known Albert for years. He had become like a father to me. Despite the fact that it could have meant my death, I told him. He said he knew and he just wanted to hear me say it.

That's when he told me what some of the antiques I collected really were. That's when he taught me how to draw the demons out of things and lock them into the hollow iron pellets.

It took me three weeks to stop thinking about the fact that I'd been driving across country with objects full of demons in the back seat of my car. Steady income tends to make you feel a lot better about questionable acts.

I worked exclusively for him for a year while I saved more than enough money for rent on an office and for the licensing to become an investigator. In that time I learned how to use conventional weapons and I took a few refresher courses in martial arts (I'd had classes as a child, because my father bought into the whole "Karate Kid" thing).

Albert cosigned my loans and my lease. He was doing it on the condition that no matter what else I was working on, his requests would take priority. He also made it clear that any vampire I encountered would be eliminated, no questions asked. His baby sister and her husband had been killed by vampires. It was their way of telling Albert to stop meddling with the supernatural. It only made Albert more determined. It was what made Albert confront me and ask me what I really was.

It was his niece, Linda Mullins, who was my contact in the local police department. She worked in the headquarters as a clerk, which meant she got to handle a lot of the paperwork that passed through the central office. Suspicious deaths, unidentified gang symbols, or any crime with unusual elements were passed to her uncle, who made the decision to forward the case to me.

I wondered how he would feel about the fact that I had a

vampire living in my house.

I never had to find out what Albert thought. They killed him.

The "They" in question wasn't immediately known. It was barely six in the morning. The only thing I was aware of, other than my extreme desire to retreat back into my dreams of chasing bunnies, was Alex. He was standing next to my bed, poking me in the shoulder and ribs.

"Nick. Nick. Nick. NickNickNickNickNick." He said my name over and over so many times he started to sound like an idling scooter. I swatted his hand away and pulled the pillow from under my head, clamping it down over my head to block him out.

"G'way!"

"Nicholas. This is Important."

I lifted the pillow and peeked out from under it. "Capital I important?"

"Capital I. Capital M. Capital portant. In italics. Are you awake enough to understand what I'm saying?"

I sat up and rubbed sleep from my eyes. "Yeah, I'm good. What's up?"

"Albert's building is on fire."

If I hadn't already been capable of understanding, I was certainly sober and wide awake now. Alex had driven to Albert's several times so I could drop off purchases. I knew he wouldn't be mistaken. Still, I had to see for myself. I got out of bed and ignored the mocking shriek from Alex as I hopped around getting into jeans and a shirt. Alex followed me back into the living room where the "breaking news" played out.

Live footage of Albert's consignment shop and attached warehouse in a blaze that we probably could have seen from the front steps. My stomach twisted in knots. Please god or whoever, please let him be safe at home. I had no idea what would happen to all of Albert's collected "things." Hopefully fire would destroy them and not release them.

I jammed on a pair of sneakers and found my keys. I tossed them to Alex, who handed me a travel mug full of hot, fresh coffee in exchange. We bolted from the house and drove to Albert's shop, weaving in and out of rush hour traffic, wishing we had a siren or some sort of official documentation to get us close to the scene.

Alex pulled into a spot two blocks from the warehouse and we ran toward the building. It was ruined. The firemen had to break down part of a wall to get inside the warehouse, which was apparently the origin of the fire. Rubble and burnt wood, dripping wet, steam rising from the ruin, and the thick smell of smoke and gasoline greeted us.

A very tall man in a heavy rubber coat greeted us next. His hand was roughly the size of my head and it clamped down on my shoulder like a steel claw, turning me away and ushering me back.

"That's my boss," I explained. "I work for him. What's happened? Is he okay?"

He wasn't okay. I could smell that he wasn't okay. He was the farthest thing from okay he could be. "Albert," I mumbled. I know I sounded pitiful, but I couldn't help it.

I sank down and sat on the curb, head in my hands, aware that the wolf was waking up. I could feel it stretching inside me, pushing my internal organs out of the way. My hands were shaking when I drew a business card from my wallet and held it out to the fireman. I couldn't lift my head. I couldn't let him see my face. Alex took the card from my fingers and passed it to the man.

The words faded in and out, drowned out by my pulse bashing into my brain. "... to contact him ... taking him home ... obviously distressed ... very close...." Then Alex's hands were under my arms and he hoisted me to my feet and steered me back in the direction of the car.

He piled me into the back seat and slid into the driver's seat, watching me in the rear view mirror. "Are we okay to drive home, or should I hide the car somewhere and let you wolf out?"

"Home," I growled. I could control it, but not for long.

Alex drove, checking me in the mirror and with quick glances over his shoulder. "It's kind of like The Hulk, huh?"

Great. Just what I needed. Another movie reference. My entire body convulsed as the wolf got stronger and tried to change my posture. I started to pull at my clothes, not wanting to be trapped in them. And, okay, not wanting to ruin my favorite jeans.

"Hold on there, pal. I don't need to get pulled over for speeding and having a half-naked man in the back seat of the car. Not again. We're almost home."

"Take my shoes off," I panted. I hoped he understood that I was going to do it and not that he should turn around and.... He turned around. "Drive, idiot!"

Fast vampire reflexes kept us from careening into a telephone pole. We were almost home. I counted my heartbeats, just to focus on something other than the searing pain. Alex got out of the car and opened the door for me, then raced ahead to open the front door to the house. I ran after him in a low crouch, hitting the floor on all fours the moment I was in the living room.

I ran for my bedroom and heard the sound of the deadbolt being slipped into place outside my door. Alex had locked me in. Vampire, two. Werewolf, zero.

Several hours later the fog lifted and I found myself on the floor of my bedroom. I was naked, cold, and confused. I sat up and started to piece together what I could remember. Fire. Albert. Dead. Gasoline, bacon, and burnt wood. Everything gone.

Someone was tapping on my door. Well, not someone. It was Alex, obviously. "Give me a sec." I struggled to my feet, every joint and muscle in my body screaming in protest, and dug through the tangle of bed sheets and clothes on the floor until I found my jeans. I pulled them on and shouted "clear" while I looked for any shirt that seemed remotely clean. Maybe I'd reconsider letting Alex into my room if I could convince him to do my laundry.

"Cops are here," he said quietly. "I told them you were in shock and I wasn't sure if you could talk to them."

"Nah, I'm fine." I shoved my fingers through my hair in a

fruitless attempt to get it back into something like order and followed Alex back to the living room. One cop sat in Alex's chair. The other on the sofa. The one on the sofa rose to shake my hand.

"We were just telling your boyfriend..." he started. Alex and I both protested. Loudly.

"Alex is just a friend! He works with me sometimes. Does the driving and helps with the heavy lifting."

"Uh-huh. Mind if I smoke? That one doesn't like it when I smoke in the car." He inclined his head toward his partner.

"Please, go right ahead. Ashtray's right there."

The cop sat back down and lit a cigarette. I sat down next to him. Alex disappeared into the kitchen. "Interesting collection of stuff," the cop said. Detective, I suppose. He was plainclothes, but his partner was in uniform.

"Yeah, I sort of got into the habit working with Albert. He'd send me out to buy something or pick up something he'd bought and I'd end up finding something for myself." Breathe, Nick. He's a detective. You're a detective. Relax.

"So what is it that you do, mister... Pardoner?"

"Well, I do pickups and buys for Albert. I started working for him in college and he helped fund my education and helped me finance my own business, so I continue to work with him. I owe him a lot."

"And your own business. What is that exactly?"

"Private investigator. Nothing high-profile. Mostly surveillance of spouses and background checks on people. It's mostly paperwork. I'm not even licensed to carry a gun." When he raised his arm to bring his cigarette to his mouth I could see the butt of the detective's gun, barely concealed under his light jacket. I hoped to God mine was locked away.

He grunted. "Know anyone that would want to hurt mister Tyson?"

"No one. He was a kind man. I've known him for years and I don't remember him ever saying anything bad about anyone or hearing him mention any trouble. His niece works for the police department, you know. She might have more information than I would."

"Ah. See, there's a small hitch. We found her body in the warehouse, too."

The world slid sideways and for one long moment I thought I was about to barf all over the detective. I pressed the back of my hand against my mouth and swallowed hard. "Guh," I said, eloquently.

The detective nodded slowly and then offered me one of his cigarettes. I accepted it gratefully. "She was a good friend to me, too. Do you have any leads at all?"

"That's why we're here mister ... Pardoner." Again the pause. I had the feeling he didn't believe it was really my name. It's not. Not by birth, but it's legally mine now. "We were hoping you could help us out."

"I want to. You have no idea how much I want to, but I honestly don't know of anyone who would want to hurt him." *Not that I could tell you about, at least. But if you're interested in tracking down any demons or vampires....*

The detective gave me a card. "Call me if you can think of anything. I'd ask you to go down to his store and see if anything's missing, but the inventory's pretty much destroyed. You might not be able to tell if anything was gone or not." We stood and shook hands. The detective and the officer let themselves out and I locked the door behind them.

They hesitated on the front step for a moment, probably assuming I couldn't hear them.

"Think he's got anything to do with it?" The officer asked.

"He nearly puked when I told him about the girl. Unless he's got some sort of Jekyll and Hyde thing going on, it wasn't him."

"Were they actually able to get an ID on the second body?" The officer again.

"Nah. They haven't found enough parts of her yet."

Alex leaned against the doorframe. "Everything cool?"

I rubbed the back of my neck and nodded. I opened my mouth to tell him what I'd just heard and ended up barfing.

"Oh, dude! You just spewed all over my shirt!"

"No, I didn't," I croaked. "That's *my* shirt. Get it off and put it in the wash. And do the rest of my laundry while you're at it."

***

Alex and I sat in the car, watching the remains of Albert's property. The arson investigators and crime scene team were still sorting through rubble. I tried not to think about the fact that they were looking for bits of Linda. I was certain they weren't going to find anything that would help them find out who did this. Now that the smell of the fire had dissipated, the smell of demons was almost overwhelming.

People from the neighborhood came up to see what was going on. A uniformed officer shooed them away. As it got later, the cops set up lights and kept working. Eventually it started to rain. Alex and I watched the crews pack up and go.

The crime scene tape pulled and jerked in the wind, reflecting the streetlights. An unattached end waved at us as we approached. I waved back without thinking about it, and Alex nudged my shoulder.

"Sure you want to do this?"

I shrugged. "It doesn't matter, does it? No one else is going to be able to catch whoever did this."

We carefully made our way to the middle of the rubble, slipping and rolling on broken stone and wet and crumbling wood. Alex nearly fell twice but caught himself before going down. It was cold and we were already soaked to the skin.

"Jesus." Alex stopped suddenly and shuddered. "What's that smell?"

"Death. Burnt human flesh. Gasoline. Destroyed antiques. Probably paint, varnish, and all sorts of molds and fungi in the air. That's why the investigators were wearing masks."

Alex covered his mouth and nose with his hands.

"You didn't have to come with me, you know." I knelt down and sifted some rocks and ash through my fingers.

"I'm here for moral support." Alex looked around, scanning the street. "And because I can keep people from seeing us."

"Don't suppose you can shield us from the rain." It was streaming down from my hair and into my eyes. I took a pinch of the silt I'd gathered and put it in my mouth.

"Oh, dude. You didn't."

I nodded and kept the sample on my tongue a little longer. I spat it out and stood up slowly.

"Xyj'Ru."

"Zidge Roo?"

"Xyj'Ru. It's a demon."

"Obviously," Alex said dryly.

I glared. "I wasn't finished. Remember you asked me what I'd do if I came across a demon that wasn't bound by iron?"

"Xyj'Ru isn't."

"He most certainly is not and we are now in very deep trouble. Xyj'Ru is one of the oldest demons around. He's not particularly powerful, but because he's nearly impossible to contain, he's gotten to be sort of..." I cast around for the right way to describe him. "If the Mafia were demons, he'd be the Godfather."

"And Albert did something to piss him off."

I nodded and toed a rock. "Might have caught him. Caught him off-guard, you know? Just long enough to bring him into the warehouse, and then the first chance he got, Xyj'Ru got even." I shoved my hands in my pockets, trying to warm them up. "Maybe Albert caught one of Xyj'Ru's children. Might be why he went after Linda, too. Maybe he started with Linda and Albert died trying to save her."

"So they really are both..." Alex swallowed hard.

"Yes."

"How do you know?"

"I can smell her. What used to be her. I can smell her and Albert." I paused. "Let's go home."

I changed into dry clothes and joined Alex on the couch. We sat side-by-side for a while, staring at the blank screen of the television. Neither of us moved, save for smoking, and neither of us spoke. In the months I'd known Alex I had never seen him so still or so quiet. I wondered what was going through his mind.

"I need to tell you something." Alex said. "I think this is my fault."

"It can't be your fault. It would either be me or Albert who brought him into the store because we're the only ones who do the retrievals. Anyhow, you've never been closer than a block away from the store until today."

Alex studied his shoes. "I know. But I've met Xyj'Ru before. He helped me out after I was turned."

I turned to face Alex and he flinched as if he expected me to hit him. Maybe he thought I was finally going to kill him. Believe me, I was thinking about it. I should have known better than to make friends with a vampire. Albert was right. You couldn't trust any of them. "Keep talking," I said as I lit another cigarette.

He drew a deep breath and let it out again in a long sigh. "So, ten years ago, I was a senior in college. It was almost the end of the fall semester and there was a massive party. I mean it was a big fucking blowout. It was the end of my last semester ever, and I figured what the hell. I'd hook up with someone, have a little fun, and then never have to see them again. One last bout of stupidity before graduating.

"So, I met this guy. Attractive. Funny. Little bit of an accent. And I invited him back to my place."

"Did he... you know. Talk you into it?" I put air quotes around "talk you into it".

"You mean charm me? I don't think he would have had to. I've always shopped in both departments, so I couldn't tell you if I was tricked into it or if it was just hormones. I mean, this guy was hot.

"Anyhow, we went to my apartment and he started biting me. I remember thinking 'well that's a fairly small kink,' and then there's a gap in my memory. The next thing I knew it was two days later, I was still in my dorm, I'd missed two finals, and there was a copy of the book Dracula on the bed and stuck to the cover was a drawing of a smiley face with fangs.

"I didn't know what to do. I hid in my room. I didn't know if I could eat. I didn't know if I could drink. I didn't know if I could go out in the sun. I didn't even move to take a piss. I stayed like that for three days. Finally I realized I was dying. I was dehydrated, hungry, and filthy because I'd been laying there pissing myself. I pulled up the window shade and I watched the sun rise and I waited for it. I waited to burst into flames or turn into ash or explode or whatever would happen. When nothing happened I just started..." He looked away from me and picked at his thumbnail. "I started crying. Begged for someone to find me and kill me."

"Instead you got Xyj'Ru."

"I should've just gone out into the hallway and pissed off some jock. Gotten my neck broken or been tossed off the roof of the building. Hindsight's twenty-twenty, right?" He laughed humorlessly. "Godfather demon is really accurate, by the way. We made a deal. He'd take care of me. Teach me to survive. Then I'd work for him. Kill on command. Instead, once I'd gotten strong enough and figured some things out on my own, I took off."

"You think he's been after you for ten years?"

"Someone like him? He'd have found me in days if he'd been looking. He... well, he did find me pretty fast. I only got away from him just before I met you."

"Why go after Albert and Linda, though? Why would he think they had any connection to you?"

Alex mumbled something.

"What did you just say?"

"I stole something from him. I stole a key. It looked like a plain old skeleton key, and it was made of wood and... I just stuck it in my pocket and left. He probably thought I gave it to Albert and was looking for it. That night in the alley -- the first night we met -- I thought you were working for Xyj'Ru and you were coming to get the key back. That's why I went to your home. That's why I asked you why you were trying to kill me. I was hoping that if he'd sent you, I could just give you the key to give back to him."

Alex looked miserable. His hair was still damp from the rain, there were shadows under his eyes, and he was chewing his lower lip. I wanted to say something. I wanted to tell him this probably wasn't his fault. That maybe Xyj'Ru had no idea about him and just went after Albert because it was likely that Albert had the key. I wanted to tell him I wasn't angry with him. Instead I said "Ganushko."

"Gesundheit."

"No, that was his name. Ganushko is the vampire that turned you." I handed my cigarette to Alex. "I killed your sire."

Alex shrugged and took a drag. "We were never close. Not even a card at Christmas." He handed the cigarette back. "I thought that if you killed the head vampire then all the other vampires would be cured."

"Vampirism is a virus. If you get the flu and kill the person who gave it to you, are you suddenly cured?"

"No, but I bet I'd still feel better. How do you know it was him?"

"The book and the note. That was actually one of the easiest kills I've ever done. It only took a little leg work to find out who'd been buying copies of Dracula in bulk."

"Did you really have to kill him?"

"He had this scheme to take over the world. He wanted to turn as many people into vampires as he could. He even kept some of his victims as recruits. Sent them out to make even more vampires."

"And they'll turn two friends, and they'll turn two friends, and so on, and so on, and so on."

"Exactly. Hey, are you okay?"

Alex shook his hair out of his eyes and smiled. "Just wondered why I wasn't good enough to be a recruit."

"Be glad you weren't. I cleaned out a nest of his underlings about a week after I took out Ganushko. You'd be dead now."

"And Albert and Linda wouldn't be dead."

We lapsed back into silence until the sound of a fire truck going down the street made me jump. "Get packed. We're getting the hell out of Dodge."

"You can't be serious."

"Alex, I realize that as far as being a vampire goes, ten years is barely out of infancy. But something you should have learned by now is that sometimes you just have to leave to protect yourself and the people around you."

Chapter Three

We threw everything we could into bags and packed them in the trunk of my car. It was almost sunrise by the time we left my place. Our first stop was my office. I grabbed my computer and my second gun. It would be useless against Xyj'Ru and I had no idea if Alex could handle it, but it wasn't something I wanted left behind. It was unregistered and I didn't have a permit for it.

See, the detective didn't give me the line about "don't leave town" but I had a feeling if he had questions and couldn't find me, my office would be tossed. Disappearing after the brutal murder of two close friends was one thing. Illegal weapons were something else entirely.

Once I was certain there was nothing incriminating left, we hit the road.

We kept it casual and drove through the morning and into the evening, stopping only for gas and very brief bathroom breaks. By the time the sun set I was starting to feel pretty good. Around midnight I was humming to myself, tapping out rhythms on the steering wheel while Alex stared through the window, half-dozing.

When it got closer to dawn, I scanned the road ahead looking for the first sign pointing to some sort of motel. Five miles to the exit. I sped up a little. The idea that we could be caught and killed at any moment was the furthest thing from my thoughts and I sang a little bit louder.

Alex started singing with me, but stopped abruptly. "Uh, you're about to be less happy." He looked over the back of the seat and pointed at the red and blue flashing lights. I pulled over.

"Y'know how fast you was goin'?" The officer spoke with a thick drawl. I heard Alex mutter something offensive about cops and I hoped he wouldn't speak any louder.

"I'm sorry, sir. We've been driving all night and we were trying to get to that exit up there." I pointed and smiled benignly. At least I hoped it was benignly.

"License and registration, please?"

"You don't need to see the registration," Alex said as he opened the glove box to reach for it.

"What you say, son?"

"Nothing. Just a joke." He passed the registration to me, I handed it to the officer. When the policeman went back to his car I glared at Alex.

"You don't need to see the registration?"

Alex shrugged. "I thought it couldn't hurt to try."

The policeman returned. He held the registration and my license between his index and middle fingers. "You know you have two unpaid parking tickets in Kentucky?"

Shit. The last pickup I did for Albert. "Yes, Officer. I'll mail a check as soon as I'm back home." My back itched as sweat rolled down it. It felt like there were ants crawling across my neck.

"I'm not gonna give you a ticket. Just watch your speed. Deer cross this highway and I've seen them fuck up a car something serious."

"Thanks. We'll be careful." I waved and watched the officer walk back to his car, then pulled out slowly. I kept a nice, steady seven-miles-under the limit for the last stretch of highway before our exit. I noticed the cruiser behind us; it wasn't until we pulled into the motel's parking lot that it continued on and away. I was tired, hungry, and I really wanted a shower. The good mood I'd been in was evaporating. At least I hadn't ended up with another ticket. "Come on. Let's get a room."

The clerk, a bored-looking old man, sneered when we came in. "Yeah?"

"We need one unit, just for a few hours. We'll be checking out about eight PM. Is there an hourly rate?"

The man held up a hand. "Full rate. You can play your dirty little sex games and keep your dirty little secret from your wives. I still get my full rate."

Alex stared at the old man, eyebrows raised in amusement. "Actually, I'm a vampire. I need somewhere to hide out until the sun sets again."

"Told you. Don't care. Seventy bucks if you pay by credit. One-forty if you pay cash."

I looked up from the newspaper I'd picked up. "What! Why?"

"In case you wreck anything. Cash, I'm covered up front. Credit, I just bill your card." He cackled at his own cleverness.

Alex pulled one hundred sixty dollars from his wallet and

slapped them down on the counter.

"Keep the change. But I'm going to destroy a chair."

The old man licked his lips and held the bills up to the light. He dropped a key on the counter. "Unit six," he murmured, still staring at the bills.

Alex sat down on the bed and picked up the television remote. Pointing it at the armchair, upholstered in a particularly unattractive shade of greenish-yellow, he announced the chair's fate. "I'll actually be doing you a favor by shredding you, chair. They might wrap you in something nicer if they choose not to let you go to the great refinisher in the sky." He pressed a button on the remote and made a zapping sound. "Either way, you win."

I shook my head and dropped my bag on the bed next to Alex. "I'm taking a shower, then I'm sleeping. I can't believe how much money we just blew on this shithole."

Alex woke me a few hours later. It was dark and the faint sound of crickets and the occasional whoosh of traffic from the highway were muffled by the nonsense Alex was babbling. Apparently, vampires can have nightmares. I couldn't understand a thing he was saying. He was speaking the secret language of dreams. Mumble, mumble, shower shoes.

Dust from the demolished seat cover caught the thin light that crept in through the poorly sealed door jamb. It had the reddish quality of sunset, so I knew we hadn't slept through the night. Although if Alex felt anything like I felt, doing that would probably be a good thing.

More mumbles and complaint sounds from the vampire. I

thought about waking him, but I was suddenly angry. It was his fault we were in this mess. It was his fault we spent almost two hundred dollars on this room. It might actually have been his fault that Albert and Linda were dead. How did I know I hadn't been tricked into this mess? I put on my shoes and went out into the parking lot.

The lot was empty aside from an ancient Ford that probably belonged to the manager. It looked like it hadn't been driven in years and might have been rusted to the spot. A blinking red light told me that there was a security system installed and I laughed out loud. Who'd even consider breaking into that pile of junk?

The only other sign of life was a plastic bag that skittered past, occasionally stopping its forward motion to swirl or leap into the air. I could still hear the sounds from the highway and the wind in the trees. *Every little breeze seems to whisper Louise*, I thought. At least I thought I thought. Turns out I'd actually sung it out loud because Alex sat down next to me and asked who Louise was.

He hunched forward and wrapped his arms across his chest, hugging himself despite the fact that it wasn't that cold. A side effect of nightmares, I guess. I don't have nightmares. I don't dream. Or if I do, I don't remember them. Alex rocked back and forth and exhaled loudly.

"I'd kill for a smoke," he said.

"I haven't got any on me, though there might still be a pack in my bag."

"Do you mind if I look? I mean, I don't want to go digging

through your personal things--"

"What personal things? It's clothes. Shirts and socks. A bunch of fucking demons in fucking iron balls. Everything that was personal got left behind." Bitter? Me? I stared at my feet and in my peripheral vision I saw him stand and turn. I heard the click of the motel room door. I hunched forward and rested my chin on my knees. What a huge fucking mess.

I saw the toes of his sneakers appear at the edge of the curb, then his feet stepped down and he sat next to me, his shoulder touching mine. I didn't look up until he nudged my shoulder and handed me the lit cigarette.

"There's about half a pack left. Figure if we share them we can make them last longer. Get another pack on our next stop."

I took it from his fingers, had a long drag, and handed it back.

"Well, they would last longer if you didn't burn half of it down at once."

"I took my half up front. The rest is yours."

The sun got lower and the breeze got stronger. The first hint of autumn was in the air and it made me shiver. I've always preferred autumn to all other times of the year but I had a bad feeling about this one.

We sat there while Alex smoked the last of the cigarette, tucked it under the toe of his shoe, and ground it out. "We should get going." I said, but made no move to stand up.

"Look, Nick, I was thinking. Now might be a good time to go our separate ways. I've gotten you into enough trouble and if I take off on my own, maybe they won't kill you. Maybe they'll get wrapped up in hunting me down that they'll forget about you, or decide they don't care anymore." He stood up and stretched, then offered me his hand. I couldn't tell if he was offering me a hand up or wanted to shake my hand goodbye.

I stood up and faced him, shoving my hands in my pockets. "It doesn't work like that. They'll keep coming after me just for helping you. Just for working for Albert. Just in case you gave the key to me. You didn't give the key to me, did you?"

"No. It's right here." He pulled out his key ring and held it up by the wooden skeleton key that I'd assumed was just a fob.

We walked back into the room and gathered up our things. Alex settled the strap of his bag across his chest and checked his pockets. "We should keep the room key just to piss that guy off."

"What's this thing you have with keeping keys? I don't think so." I held out my hand for the motel room key and Alex dropped it in my upturned palm. We ignored the stares from the clerk when we returned it. Let people think what they want. That's my general rule. Nothing they could make up could be anywhere near the truth.

"Hey," started Alex as we pulled out of the motel parking lot, "do you think if we gave Xyj'Ru the key back he'd let us go?"

I counted seventeen seconds before he spoke again. "No, huh."

***

The truck stop restaurant was packed with drivers getting ready to start their day. They put away eggs and pancakes and steak and ham. The whole place smelled of bacon, coffee, and maple syrup. Hunger battled with exhaustion. I hadn't realized just how hungry I was until we were actually faced with food. I touched the wallet in my front pocket and wondered how much longer the money would hold out.

We were seated in a booth tucked in a corner near the kitchen. Our waitress was a girl whose tag read Anna. The sea foam-green waitress uniform looked good against her olive-toned skin and drew attention to the fact that her eyes were a pale blue (on the other waitress, middle-aged, fleshy, and pale, it only made her look ill). Alex and I exchanged a glance when we noticed the silver crucifix that hung from a thin chain around Anna's throat. Alex smirked slightly and rolled his eyes.

"Good morning, gentlemen, and what can I get you for breakfast?" Her voice was warm and friendly, the complete opposite of the other waitress' phlegmy, raspy voice.

"I'll have the lumberjack platter and coffee. And your phone number." Alex gave her a smooth wink. She rolled her eyes, but laughed.

"How do you want your eggs, sir?" She was good. A complete professional.

"Scrambled. No, wait. Over light. But make the bacon extra-crispy." He looked at me and said "There's less grease that way. It burns off." He patted his stomach. "Can't afford any extra fat, you know."

It was my turn to roll my eyes. Alex, despite a healthy appetite, was thin. He had almost no body fat and had definite muscle tone despite the fact that I never saw him working out. I don't have that sort of luck. I ordered a steak (rare) and an egg-white omelet. Alex made a little gagging noise. The idea of not having yolks repulsed him. The onions and green peppers I asked to be included made him cringe.

"Onions and green peppers?" He hissed at me once Anna the waitress had gone to put our order in.

"I like onions and green peppers!"

"You don't have to deal with onion breath in your face afterwards."

"I won't breathe on you."

"I wish I could believe you."

"Oh come on. My onion breath can't be as bad as your Kung Pao Incident."

"*My* Kung Pao incident? That's great, coming from you, mister Burrito Night."

"I told you not to put so many beans in th--" Our argument was cut short when Anna returned with two mugs of coffee and a little dish of creamer tubs. She had an odd sort of smile on her face as she put the things down.

"Gentlemen, your breakfasts will be out in a few minutes. Just give me a call if you need more coffee or if I can get anything else for you."

"I'd still like your phone number?" Alex asked.

"Oh, you!" She laughed lightly and touched Alex's shoulder before she walked away.

"I think she likes me."

I leaned across the table and whispered to him. "I think she thinks we're gay."

"I call bullshit."

"No bullshit. I think she thinks we're gay! I'm telling you. Watch. Listen!"

Anna was talking to the man at the cash register. Her posture had shifted slightly and she looked a little less perky. A line creased Alex's forehead as he listened to their conversation, inaudible to anyone else because of the din around us. "--seems really nice and he's kind of cute, but I think they're-- you know. A couple." She gestured quotes when she spoke the words "a couple."

Alex slumped back in his seat and tapped his spoon against the table. "Well, fuck me."

"That'd really confirm her suspicions." I hid my smirk behind my coffee and ducked the spoon that came flying at my head.

After breakfast, we had time to kill. Baltimore was only a few hours away at this point, but we were both tired. Rather than waste more cash at another motel, we opted to slum it for one night. Alex marveled at the fact that I don't carry credit cards. I pointed out that he didn't even have a bank account.

Vampire, two. Werewolf, one.

I took my computer and used the truck stop's wireless connection to send money from my bank account to a Western Union pickup in Baltimore. Our half-baked plan was to take the key and see if I could figure out what was so important about it. Remember I said that Xyj'Ru wasn't bound by iron? Maybe the key unlocked the one thing that could contain him. One thing I was certain of; it wasn't sentimental value that drove him to find the key. Demons don't do sentimental. Except around the holidays, when sentiment can make people angry.

So we slummed it in the trailer section of an eighteen-wheeler parked in the truck stop lot. Aside from a few cardboard boxes that had been flattened (possibly by previous "tenants" of these four-star, luxury accommodations) it was empty. The cab wasn't connected and judging by the amount of trash that had built up around the tires of the trailer, it hadn't been moved in a while.

"It's not exactly a room at the Ritz," Alex said as he stood in what was roughly the center and turned in a small circle to take in his surroundings.

"We're not exactly dressed for the Ritz." I put our bags down in a corner and stretched. "It's shelter. And it's only temporary. Just for one night. It's better than trying to sleep in the car."

"Your fault for buying a Jetta. Next time get something like a Buick. Much roomier for living in." Alex tied a sock to the handle on one door and pulled them both shut, wedging the sock between them so they didn't meet flush. He tested to ensure that they could be opened again.

"You might have waited until I'd gone outside," I said. Our voices were hollow and echoed in the large, empty, metal box. "What if that hadn't worked and we were shut in here?"

A shaft of sunlight squeaked between the two doors and cut a sharp diagonal across his face. He flashed a grin and slammed the doors closed completely.

"Are you out of your fucking mind?" Something like terror rose in my throat. I suddenly regretted the onions and green peppers. A badass demon was after him and he potentially locked us in a metal box that wasn't going to keep it out. We were, at that moment, sitting ducks.

Alex crossed to the far end of the trailer and made a run for the door, slamming into it with his shoulder. The doors popped open and he grabbed wildly, catching the edge of one of them and laughing gleefully as he swung back and forth before the door finally came to rest against the back of the trailer. He stepped back inside, panting and red-faced. "How about that!" He was giddy.

"Well, that was certainly noisy." I stared at him, nonplussed. "Did that demonstration have a point?"

"No. Well, it was fun. But I was just testing."

"Testing to see what it would take for me to actually want to kill you?"

Alex went to the front of the trailer again and sat down on one of the squashed boxes. He leaned against the wall and took his shoes off, putting them next to his bag. He was sulking.

I sat down on the edge of the trailer, letting my legs dangle over the edge. "Nothing like watching the morning sun cast its cheery glow over the Dumpster."

"That's like fucking poetry," Alex said, his words bouncing around the container before reaching me. He might have been speaking from miles away. I heard the nearly-silent whisper of his bare feet padding across the floor. He sat down beside me and lit a cigarette. "And look! There's rats." He handed the cigarette to me.

"You know what bothers me?" Alex said. "The word 'immortal.' I'm not immortal. It seems like the word has started to mean 'really hard to kill.' I mean, if I were immortal we wouldn't be doing this, right? I'd just stand up and say, 'Bitch, I'm immortal! I can't die!' and have Xyj'Ru for lunch. But I can't do that. I'm not immortal. I'm not even really hard to kill. I'm probably incredibly easy to kill." He sighed, his shoulders drooping.

We continued to pass the cigarette back and forth. "How come you haven't killed me? I mean, I'm completely responsible for this."

"You make a good point. Do you want to die now, or tomorrow morning?"

"No, seriously, Nick. Why haven't you killed me?"

"Wolves are pack animals. They need the company of others. It's one of the reasons why dogs were so easy to domesticate. Shifters are no different; at least not the wolf shifters. The people who shift to solitary animals are usually fine on their own."

"So why not just find a whole flock of other wolf shifters and live communally ever after?"

"Pack."

"Whatever. You're avoiding the question again."

"I did, actually. On one of my trips for Albert, out in New

Mexico. They were already a family, though. They had their alphas and their pack order and I wasn't willing to start at the bottom and fight my way up. You can't have two alpha males in a pack and the others were very willing to protect their leader's position. It would have been seven against one and I didn't like the odds." I omitted the part about hating being a shifter at all. I skipped telling him that I couldn't stand myself, so why would I want to be around others like me? Judging by the sly smile he was giving me I had a hunch he already knew it.

"So you haven't killed me because you were lonely."

"Shut up, Alex."

***

Our next destination was yet another truck stop not far outside of the downtown Baltimore area. The air was heavy with humidity and smelled of ozone and diesel exhaust. The skyline of downtown Baltimore wavered in the distance. I could almost smell the water. It smelled dirty and fishy. The overpowering smell, the one that cut through all the others, was the greasy French fry scent from the fast food place down the hill from where we stood.

Alex yawned, slung one arm around my neck, and planted a kiss on my cheek. "I'm hungry." "What, again?" Alex was a bottomless pit. I didn't know if the fact that he wasn't regularly feeding on blood meant he was always hungry for something or if he'd been that way before he was turned. He was living in a sort of prolonged adolescence in just about every other way.

"I'm always hungry!" he called back to me as he started in the direction of the restaurant. "Are you coming or not? You'd better be, because you've got the cash."

I pulled out my wallet and counted the bills, then looked around the parking lot. I wondered if there was time to get the money from the Western Union pickup. Alex was already at the door to the restaurant. The money would have to wait.

I caught up with Alex inside, at the counter. He'd already placed the order and was just waiting patiently for me to show up with the cash. He grinned sunnily. I thought about punching him.

I paid. We ate and watched the cars going by on the interstate. I used a fry to draw in the ketchup on his burger wrapper and thought about what we'd do next. Get the cash. Get a room. Take a shower. Sleep in a real bed.

Wolf or not, I'm a civilized guy and I like having a shower that works, a toilet that flushes, and my own coffee maker. And my own room. I don't really enjoy the thought of sleeping with a vampire who keeps kicking me in the shins because he's having a nightmare. I was not made for that sort of lifestyle.

It turned out that we were at a combination bus station, truck stop, and hotel. The Western Union was in the bus station. The brochures in the hotel lobby told us how to get to the zoo, the aquarium, the best places to eat, and told us we were very near a train station. There was, the hotel's brochure boasted, also a shuttle to get to the hospital quickly.

Some or all of this information might turn out to be useful. I folded up the stack of fliers and put it in my jeans pocket.

While I was browsing, Alex was busy chatting up the desk clerk. He sauntered over, looking pleased with himself and handed me a hotel key card. "One king-size bed, twenty-five inch television, smoking room, coffee maker, hairdryer for drying your shaggy ass, and a complimentary buffet breakfast."

"How did you... I didn't give you any money. You didn't... 'you know'," I waggled my fingers, "the girl, did you?"

"I didn't 'you know' her." He waggled his fingers back at me. "I will need you to be out of the room tonight, for about two hours."

"So you didn't..." I waggled my fingers again. "But you will..." I made an entirely different gesture.

Alex nodded and tapped the side of his nose. I squeezed the bridge of mine and tried to think happy thoughts.

Several hours later, I was sitting in a very dark corner in a very dark bar drinking a very warm beer. It was my third and I'd been nursing it not out of any attempt to remain sober but because I couldn't afford to drink as much as I wanted.

The vinyl seat crackled every time I moved, the floor was sticky, and the jukebox seemed to contain only Lynyrd Skynyrd and Def Leppard. A skinny man with lank hair in a thin ponytail played pinball. I took a long drink of the warm, flat beer and sighed. My happy place was drifting away again. I signaled the waitress and ordered a double shot of Scotch.

When I got back to the hotel I knocked quietly, then unlocked the door. I hoped Alex would have had enough sense to put the chain on the door if he were still busy with his "date."

The door clicked and swung open easily and I stepped in with my eyes half-closed, using the mirror on the closet door to scope as much of the room as possible.

Alex was curled up asleep in the middle of the bed. He was dressed, save for his shoes and his left sock. His hair looked damp, and when I stepped into the bathroom I confirmed that he had showered recently. The mirror was still foggy.

I peed and then wiped a clear spot above the sink with the palm of my hand. "You look like hell, Nicky."

"Don't call him Nicky. He hates that." Alex slurred from the bed. The springs creaked as he rolled off the mattress and padded over to stand behind me. "Whoa. You look like hell, Nicky. Who were you talking to?"

"No one. Just myself. Alex. What are you doing?"

What he was doing was nuzzling the side of my neck, just below my ear. I couldn't tell if the prickling along the base of my skull was vampire influence or his breath. Either way, it had to stop.

I gripped his shoulders and pushed him away from me, leaning him against the bathroom wall.

"Alex. What are you doing?"

He opened one eye and sighed. "Nothing. Good night, Nick." He shuffled back to bed and curled up around one of the pillows, his back to the door.

I made sure the "do not disturb" card was on the handle, then locked it and put the chain on. I kicked off my shoes and crawled into bed, my back to Alex's.

When I woke up, I found him sitting in the chair by the window, a cup of coffee on the arm and muffin crumbs on his shirt. He was clutching a doughnut in one hand and a banana in the other. "Balanced diet," he said and took a bite from each one and chewed them together. Once the doughnut was gone he picked up the coffee. It looked like Alex had collected the entire complimentary breakfast buffet and deposited it in our room.

"Potassium. That's your problem. Not enough of it. Have some banana!" When he spoke he gestured at me with the banana. I curled up into a ball and put a pillow over my head. This didn't stop him. He climbed onto the bed and knelt next to me, tapping my shoulder with the side of his fist. "Ba-na-na. Ba-na-na. Ba-na-na." He chanted.

"Alex," I grumbled into the pillow.

"Ba-na-na!"

"Alex!" I shouted into the pillow.

"Ba-na-na!"

"ALEX!"

"What!"

I grabbed the pillow and smacked him with it, breaking his precious banana in half. "You are a vampire!"

"Yes!"

"You're supposed to be nocturnal. Do you know what that means?"

"I ... do stuff at night?"

"Precisely. Therefore, you should not be a morning person." He blinked stupidly at me. "I am not a morning person, Alex. I am not a morning person on my good days. I am even less of a morning person when I've been getting drunk in a bar until closing time because you needed to get laid!"

"Well, I didn't *need* to get laid." He picked up the broken banana and finished eating it.

"You are not helping your situation."

"Okay. Okay. I get it. I'm sorry. I was rude, inconsiderate, and I should be punished." He slid off the bed and turned around, sticking his butt out at me. "Right there. Come on. Just belt me a good one."

I grabbed the pillow again and smacked him. Then I laughed. It felt like it had been months since I'd laughed, even though it had probably only been a day or two. My life had turned into something completely and utterly absurd, so what else could I do? It was either laugh or cry, and crying wouldn't get anything done. I smacked him again and again. Eventually he grabbed the other pillow and started hitting back. We didn't stop until we were exhausted and breathless.

Chapter Four

Fell's Point is a historic district that is almost entirely kitschy shops, bars, and tourists. I'd already spent several hours drinking in one of the more out-of-the-way bars in the area, putting out feelers for news and information. I listened intently to conversations. I watched the people and scanned the faces of everyone that glanced in my direction. I studied the people who made a point of not looking at me.

Alex went to Fell's Point with me on our second night in Baltimore. We stood on the end of a pier, looking out at a giant neon sign. I was breathing shallowly. Alcohol, vomit, food, perfume, sweat, piss and shit, both human and animal. Fumes from the cars and the boats. The garbage-and-fish smell of the water. Everything I'd smelled back at the hotel. Everything I'd smelled the night before. Everything I hated about humanity. Alex embraced it all. In this case, he literally embraced it. He stood on the wooden rail that edged the pier and spread his arms to let the night wind blow his hair and jacket. He closed his eyes and sighed contentedly.

"Why here?" he asked. "Baltimore, I mean."

"Call it a hunch."

He hopped down and shoved his hands in the pockets of his jacket. "Have you ever been here before?" He cocked his head to one side and patted himself down for cigarettes. I handed him the pack I was carrying; Alex lit two and handed me one.

"Yeah, once. A long time ago. Just a few days on a pickup." There was just something about this place. I'd been here on retrieval and felt it then, before I really understood what it was I was feeling.

Older cities and anywhere with a violent history usually have a high number of what I learned to call "hot spots." Hubs of supernatural activity. Places where things like ley lines cross or there's a thin space between the real world and the spirit world. Places that are very, very old or have a violent and bloody past. Take a place like Baltimore that combines crossed lines, age, and violence and it's prime location for a hot spot. Fell's Point even boasted about it, offering (for a price) a "ghost walk" that would take you around the area and show you the ghosts' favorite haunts. Pun intended.

Anyhow, hot spots are usually a big draw for people like us. Well, I couldn't speak for Alex. I didn't know how much territory a vampire needed and if "overcrowding" was a problem among his kind. I wasn't even sure if there were any other vampires in the area.

My fingers itched to touch a keyboard and find out if the Dayton police were looking for me. Find out if there were any "things" like us around. I wondered how serious Xyj'Ru was about finding us.

Alex paced back and forth. His head was down and there was a look of concentration on his face that I had rarely (possibly never) seen before. I inhaled through my nose and mouth and couldn't pick up anything, but I had no idea if his senses were sharper than mine, or if he was tuned into something I couldn't detect at all. I still had three of the iron balls in the pocket of my jacket. If I needed them, I knew I could use them. What was he tracking?

"Kimmy loves Bobby forever. Twelve, twelve, oh-two. Aww. Ooh, wait. Kimmy loves Marc-with-a-C. Also forever. Four, twenty-five, oh-five. I wonder if that's the same Kimmy?" Alex looked up at me, the glowing end of his cigarette bobbing as he spoke.

"Reading the bricks," he said in answer to my unspoken question. Mystery solved. My highly supernatural and oh-so-special friend was only reading the dedications molded into the pavement. I would have sighed if I hadn't been so unsurprised.

"Alexander, are you aware of anything?"

"In general, or were you asking about something specific?"

This did make me sigh. "Sometimes I wonder. I meant can you tell if there's anything like us around."

Alex cocked his head to one side again and appeared to be listening to something. He squinted, wrinkled his forehead, and pursed his lips. "I'm going to have to go with no. I can't even tell you're like us and I know you."

I raised my eyebrows, genuinely surprised. I thought about our meeting in the alley the first night. He demanded to know what I was and dodged the question when I asked him if he could tell. "You really can't, can you."

He shook his head and shrugged. "Guess not. Maybe I just haven't learned how. It's not something I ever thought I'd need, I guess."

"You never wondered about finding other vampires? You never needed to keep yourself safe from other... others?"

Alex offered me his one-shoulder shrug. "What about you? You hunt them. You knew I was one. Can't you pick up on anything?"

"I can only tell by looking at them. If I know one's around I go where they were last seen and look around until I spot one."

"That's not very practical, is it?"

"It's worked so far."

***

We spent three days in the hotel before guilt started to build up. Guilt, and the start of the weekend, which meant a different set of staff and the reality that someone would realize we weren't being billed. Alex and I slipped out quietly in the middle of the night, leaving the room nearly immaculate. Alex stole towels, soaps, and shampoo from a maid's cart and even made an attempt to put the little fold in the toilet paper that indicated housekeeping had been in there.

"Too bad we can't wipe their memories," Alex whispered as we made our way through the halls.

He waved his right hand in a subtle gesture. "These are not the men you're looking for."

"Life isn't like the movies," I muttered back as we slipped out through the doorway that led to the bus terminal. This section wasn't what I'd call buzzing with activity, but there were signs of life. People sat on duffel bags waiting to board their buses. Old men dressed in tattered clothes clustered around the wobbly tables, nursing coffees and sodas. Bored janitors moved back and forth sweeping nothing into dustpans. We crossed through the "food court" and stepped out of the building.

The night was cool, but humid. It was hard to decide if I wanted to shiver or sweat. I chose to do both. Alex wasn't bothered. I suppose it's one of the up-sides of being a vampire.

We had nothing better to do so we walked the route to Fell's Point. The bars would be closed but there would still be bored kids reluctant to go home and people without homes to go to. Maybe Alex could find a snack or two. I had no idea when he'd last fed. If nothing else, there was at least one twenty-four hour diner. That would keep us occupied for a while; give us time to think.

We were given no time to think. We were rounding a corner when a feeling of overwhelming dread came over me. I glanced sideways at Alex and watched color drain from his face. "We're fucked, aren't we?" Alex murmured, barely opening his mouth. We stood frozen like statues, afraid that even a movement as simple as breathing would bring down whatever it was.

The fear was like a fog. It was working itself into my clothes and the pores of my skin and worming into my brain. I started breathing harder. The streetlights seemed to take on a reddish tint. Alex's hands were clenched into fists and he squeezed his eyes shut tight. I wanted to kill him. I wanted to tear his throat out with my teeth. I could envision myself shoving my thumbs into his eyes until I felt them pop. My head was filled with a hundred situations involving Alex torn to shreds. Judging by the look on Alex's face, he was having similar thoughts about me. He grinned and I could see the tips of his fangs. We stood facing each other. I crouched slightly, wondering if the wolf was going to be pulled from me or if we'd do this man against man.

Alex's foot shot out. He was much faster than I'd expected. Much faster than he'd ever shown me before. The side of his heel connected with my temple and knocked me sideways. I grabbed for his leg as it continued past, but by the time my hands were up, he was standing in front of me, balanced and ready to spring if I moved toward him.

We circled each other. He bounced on his toes and I crouched, almost crawling. I blocked another kick but couldn't hold on long enough to pull him to the ground. He grabbed my wrist and hauled me to my feet. Fists flew. I could feel my hands connecting with Alex's body but he took each punch and gave back as good as he got. One blow caught me full in the face and I felt my lip split against my teeth. The anger drained like someone had pulled the plug in a bathtub.

I spat. My blood smacked against Alex's cheek. "That's gross," he hissed and drew back his hand to hit me again. Then the smell of the blood broke through whatever had fogged his brain. He touched his cheek and looked at his fingers. Then he looked at me. I spat again (into the gutter this time) and pressed the back of my arm against my mouth. My mouth throbbed every time my heart beat and my lip was bleeding heavily.

He used his sleeve to wipe my blood from his face. "I can..." Alex stammered, indicating my split lip. "I can do something about that. You won't like it, though."

I knew what he could do. My face got hot. That just made everything hurt more. I tried to sigh but ended up coughing on the blood I swallowed. I nodded and closed my eyes, bracing myself for what would come next.

"Not here," Alex said. He took hold of my sleeve and pulled me toward a breezeway between two houses. It was barely wide enough for the two of us to stand face-to-face. Alex put his hands on either side of my face to keep me from turning my head. "Just trust me," he said as he leaned in close.

"I don't really have a choice, do I?"

"Not really, no."

His nose brushed against mine and I felt his tongue tracing my lower lip. It nudged gently against the corner of my mouth and left a wet trail along my chin. Alex's tongue was slightly rough, like a cat's tongue, and probably for much the same reason. I held my breath. The hairs on the back of my neck started to rise, so I tapped Alex on the shoulder. "None of that, please."

"Sorry," he muttered against my cheek. He pulled back and even in the dark alley I could tell he was eyeing me critically. "It's swollen. I can't do anything about that. But the bleeding has stopped and it shouldn't hurt as much." He wiped his mouth with the back of his hand.

"Thank you."

Alex laughed. "No, thank you. I've never had shifter before. That was high test." He peeked out of the alley. "It's clear. Let's go get something to eat."

Alex ordered while I locked myself in the tiny, dark restroom of the Drunken Sailor and washed my face. The water smelled sharp and metallic, but it was cold and clean. I looked like a man who had been punched in the face, but I wasn't bleeding. I joined Alex in the shabby dining area. He pushed an order of fries and a foam cup of soda into the center of the table. He handed me a cheeseburger and unwrapped his own.

We ate in silence. The electric clock that hung over the grill ticked out the seconds and a fat man in a greasy chef's jacket wiped down the counter with a rag that had been sitting in a pan of grayish water. He hummed and thankfully kept to himself. It was probably the fact that we looked like we'd been in a fight that made him keep his distance, but I wasn't going to encourage him to chat. Alex and I had business to discuss.

"What happened out there?" I asked.

Alex frowned and chewed his food. He reached over and touched my left cheekbone. "You're going to have a black eye."

"Yes, I'm aware of that. Thank you. Now focus, Alex. What happened to us?"

He shrugged one shoulder and took another bite of his burger. "Possession, I suppose. Something passed through us and upped our anger levels."

"What was it, though?"

"I don't know. You're the brains. I'm just the looks, remember?"

"It wasn't a vampire."

"Not my sort, anyhow. Psychic? Something that'd feed off the aggression? Or needed blood that it couldn't get on its own, so it makes people draw blood." He floundered as he tried to find the word he wanted. "Non-corporeal!"

I gestured, indicating that Alex needed to keep his voice down. He looked apologetic. "You're on to something. But what is it?"

"What's it matter? Do you really think it's a good idea to go after it, Nicky? I mean, we don't want to draw attention to ourselves."

"Someone's got to do something about it." Out on the street, an ambulance and two police cars shrieked past. People who weren't us had been inspired to violence by the unseen force.

"Why us, though? We've got nowhere to stay, almost no weapons, limited access to cash...."

The man behind the counter let out a long, slow sigh. "Okay. Which one of you is the vampire?" he asked. For the second time that night, Alex went completely pale.

Alex and I broke for the door. Alex got there first and tried to shove it open. The cook had locked it. Alex threw himself at it again and the metal started to pull away from the frame. I stood between Alex and the cook, ready to attack. The cook didn't move an inch. He just stood behind the counter, meaty arms folded across his broad chest, and a thin trickle of sweat running down the side of his face. He shook his head, ran one hand across his buzzed scalp, and lowered himself onto a stool behind the counter.

"Y'all going to buy me a new door if you don't stop that."

On his fourth go at the door, Alex pulled back and thunked against the thick Plexiglas. He lightly beat his forehead against it, muttering "no" over and over again. I backed up against him. Two against one. The guy was old, in poor health, and unless he had an assault rifle behind the cash register, I was certain we could take him.

Please don't let him have an assault rifle behind the cash register, I begged whatever might be listening.

"You could bounce open the truck, but you couldn't get through this?" I hissed.

"That was older, in bad shape, and wasn't locked" he murmured back.

The cook continued to stare at us. "Well?" He asked again. "Which one of you is the vampire?"

"Maybe he's not a threat," I said.

"Maybe he is," Alex replied.

"Maybe he's in the room and can hear you," the cook said.

The cook's name was Buck. He said he had worked in this restaurant for four years and he was familiar with whatever it was that had put us at odds. He said they called it Howler. When it would drift through the neighborhood it'd make all the dogs bark and howl. If it came across any people it would encourage them to fight until blood was shed.

"I don't know if it likes the blood or the fight," Buck explained, "but it ain't uncommon here.

There's a fight almost every night. Sometimes they end with the cops showing up. Sometimes ol' Howler gets distracted and lets them go before they cause too much damage. But it happens. At least once a night it'll happen. Sometimes more, depending."

"Depending on...?" I coaxed.

Buck shrugged. "Weather? Time of day? How much blood it got the night before?"

"Why'd you ask which one of us was a vampire?" Alex asked.

"Heard Barb's dog barking up the street. Knew that meant Howler was out somewheres, then you two come in here looking like you've just been in a war. Neither of you was bleeding, but that gash on his lip," he pointed to me, "should have been gushing like a busted faucet."

"So naturally you assumed one of us was a vampire." Alex raised one eyebrow.

"Wouldn't you?"

"Do you get a lot of vampires around here?" I touched the back of my neck, hoping that Alex would pick up on the signal I was trying to give him. *Charm him. Enchant him. Do whatever it takes so we can get out of here.* I felt like I was screaming it, but the word seemed to sail past Alex.

"Not as many as we used to. One or two every year, maybe." He spoke very matter-of-factly, as if he were describing the weather.

"And, uh--" I cleared my throat. "And what do you do with these vampires?"

"Me? Nothing. Ain't my business. They come, they go, that's it. Maybe a few people go missing, but that happens all the time. Kids run away from home. Wives leave husbands. Husbands leave wives. People die from perfectly normal homicide." He shrugged his beefy shoulders. "Long as they don't bother me and mine, I don't care."

"So, if someone came in here and asked if you'd seen two people like, oh, let's say us, just for the sake of example. If someone came in here asking about us, what would you tell them?"

"Depends. What you going to do about my door?"

As it turned out, the worst thing that happened to the door was some of the paint was flaked off and there were fingerprints (and forehead prints) on the glass. Alex took a rag and some window cleaner and took care of that.

Once Alex had done his penance, the three of us sat down at a booth with a pot of coffee and several very stale doughnuts. "Tell us about this Howler thing," I said while Alex loaded his coffee with powdered creamer and sugar.

Charles "Buck" Whitmore spread his fat fingers on the table. "I don't know what else to tell you. It's only at night, usually after two in the morning when the bars are closed. If you're out by yourself it can't do much to you. Might make you go look for a fight, but if you can't find one, it's got to move on. It don't ever seem to go much outside this area. Like I ain't never heard of it in Dundalk or even Little Italy. Just mostly Fell's Point and Canton, right down here at the water.

Maybe up at the park."

"Do you have a map of the area?"

"There might be a street map in the cabinet under the cash register somewhere." He started to unwedge himself from the bench, but Alex stood first.

"I'll look. You talk." Alex said.

Alex found one that was fairly old. Buildings had been put up or torn down in the time since the map was drawn, but the street names were the same. That was fine with me. I wasn't looking for an address; I was establishing a territory.

"You seriously want to go after this thing?" Alex whispered in my ear while Buck marked off boundaries on the map.

"We can't leave this thing roaming around," I responded just as quietly. One of the first things we learned while working together is that we've both got extra-sensitive hearing. The lowest mumble comes through loud and clear, almost telepathically, especially when we're sitting very close together.

"Sure we can!" Alex used his chin to gesture at the map. "Look, it's not a big area at all. Easy enough to avoid!"

"*We* can avoid it, but what about the people that live here?"

"They've lived with it for who knows how long. They'll be fine."

"I can't do it. I can't work like that."

"We've got Xyj'Ru to worry about. We've got a key that needs a lock. My life is in danger already and you want to stop a bunch of dicks from beating each other up on the weekends. You know what your problem is, Nicky? You're too fucking noble."

Alex actually shouted 'You're too fucking noble'. Buck looked up and squinted at us. "D'you mind?" He shoved the map across the table, turning it to face us. "That's it. Roughly. Some places I just don't know no one, or just never heard nothing, so I can't be sure."

It was a relatively small area, running from the water to the far side of the park, and to something he'd marked "The

Underpass" to the edge of downtown, right where an interstate began. Very clear boundaries, at least. This didn't mean it couldn't leave the marked area. As Buck had so elegantly stated, "he never heard nothing". But it gave us an idea of where we were likely to find it.

The next step would be finding out what "it" really was.

Actually, I tell a lie. The next step was finding somewhere to sleep. The next, next step would be finding out what it really was, after a good night's (well, morning's) rest and something other than stale doughnuts and burnt coffee to eat. Buck offered us crash space in his house. The "club basement," he said, would be the perfect place for us.

We waited at the restaurant a few more hours. Alex swept up and did a few dishes. I counted cracks in the Formica tabletop and used the undetermined stains on the ceiling like stars, creating constellations. I was just about to name The Great Splot of Understanding when the door opened and a scrawny guy in jeans and a T-shirt came in and called a greeting to Buck.

"Awright, Bucky," he said as he went around behind the counter and tied on an apron. He was so skinny the belt wrapped around his waist twice before tying in the back. "Quiet night?"

"Yeah, 'cept for these two. Howler made a pass at 'em. Let them wait here until the sun started coming up. We'll get out from under your feet."

Buck stepped carefully to the sidewalk, already wheezing with the exertion of going down a step. I hoped he didn't live far, because I didn't think Alex and I could carry him home. Not even with above-average strength on our side.

It was not a long walk. Just up to the far corner, around, and two blocks toward the park. We were about one block east of where we bumped into Howler. No wonder he knew so much about it.

Alex and I hung back while he carefully worked his way up the three steps to his front door. The screen door wasn't locked. The storm door behind it opened into a vestibule. There was one more door – wood with stained glass – that opened into the house, almost directly into the stairs to the second floor.

Buck went to the kitchen and poured a glass of water. "Want anything?" our host offered.

"Just sleep," I said. I knew Alex was hungry again - it must've been minutes since he ate – but I wanted to rest and then get started looking for Howler. Buck indicated the stairs to the basement.

We marveled at the utter tackiness of the room. Shag carpet. Dark, wood paneling. A drop, fiberboard ceiling. The sofa was brown, ugly, itchy, and pulled out into a double bed. There was a yellow and brown afghan and several home-crocheted pillows "decorating" it.

I'm sure there were other crimes against nature and interior design, but I didn't notice most of them and didn't care about the rest. I set to work moving furniture and pulling out the sofa while Alex took a long look around.

"I was worried this might be a trap," he said. "That he'd get us here and then sneak down and kill us. Now I think I'd like to die rather than wake up and see this again."

I kicked off my shoes and crawled into the bed. "That can be arranged."

***

Buck didn't kill either of us and I still didn't get around to killing Alex. Instead, we slept for a few hours and then went back into Fell's Point. I'd seen a sign offering free wi-fi in several of the bars, so I took my computer and we settled in for an afternoon of drinking and research. Two good things that go great together.

Alex sat across from me, using my mobile phone to play games, asking and answering questions as needed. He was also in charge of keeping the beers and snacks coming.

The plan was simple. Now that we knew what to look for, all we'd have to do is wait for it to go hunting, then draw it into one of the iron balls. The trouble would be figuring out where it was hunting. While the territory it covered wasn't huge, it was still more than two men could cover on foot.

Driving, we'd miss feeling it. We had to be outside, where we could be in it.

When Buck went back to work that night, I sat down at the counter and outlined my plan.

"Won't work," he said as he dumped fries into the wire basket.

"Why not?"

"It's touched you once. I don't think it's ever gone for the same people twice. Maybe it can't.

Maybe it only gets one shot and then your body don't fall for it again."

"Demonic immunity," Alex said. He was watching the progress of the fries into the hot oil. He was practically drooling.

"So, we need bait." I shrugged.

Buck shook his head and shook the basket of fries. "Don't even look at me. I had my run-in with Howler about six years ago. 'S why I don't mind working here."

The idea of roping anyone else into this, especially when we didn't know anyone in the city, was out of the question. That left only one option.

"We'll just have to wander around until we see a fight, I guess. Maybe get a little portable police scanner. See where the emergency services are going and hope we can get there in time."

This time, Alex shook his head. "Remember what happened to us? By the time the cops come, Howler will be gone. He takes off once there's blood spilled."

My simple plan suddenly got a lot more complicated. We had no choice but to roam around and hope we'd be in the right place at the right time. I slapped a five dollar bill on the counter. "Give Alex those fries in a to-go cup, and add two sodas. We're going to be out a while. We'll meet you back here at the end of your shift."

Buck flipped a salute and dumped the fry basket into the warming tray. He piled fresh, salty fries into a foam clamshell and filled two waxed paper cups with cola. "Good luck, guys."

"So how come you trust him?" Alex asked through a mouthful of fries.

"Don't really have much of a choice, do I? He knows what you are and he knows what we're looking for. He's nice enough. He's gone out of his way for us for no reason. I get a good vibe from him, too."

"You just operate on instinct, don't you? You just sniff out who's good and who's evil?"

"And what's a demon, and who's a vampire." I shot him a sideways glance. "It hasn't failed me yet."

"You ever kill anyone by mistake? Like exorcise someone and have them die, or wolf out and..." He made a clawing gesture in the empty air.

My face got hot. This wasn't a conversation I was ready to have, but since he brought it up, I figured it was best to get things out in the open. I took a deep breath, and then exhaled slowly. "Actually, yes. I killed my father."

Alex stopped walking and stared open-mouthed at me. "The fuck you say!"

I spread my hands and shrugged. "You asked."

"How? When?" He backed up a step. "Why?"

"Come on, Alex."

We walked into the park and up a hill. Eventually we stood next to a pagoda that seemed very out of place in the middle of an American city. Alex wandered around in small circles, staring up at the sky. I sat down and leaned against the fence that surrounded the pagoda. I lit a cigarette and watched the smoke rise and pull apart in the breeze.

"I was seventeen. It was just before I left home. It was *why* I left home. And it was an accident. I'd locked myself in my room. I was doing that a lot because I was terrified I'd wolf out at the wrong time. My dad assumed... I guess he thought I was doing drugs because I would turn my stereo up loud and take my phone off the hook. One night he let himself into my room and..." I made the clawing gesture.

Alex stopped pacing and stared down at me. Then he motioned for the cigarette. He took a long drag, held it, and then exhaled smoke through pursed lips. "What about your mother?" He asked finally.

"She died when I was ten. Cancer."

"What'd you do? After you...."

"Killed him? I ate him."

The expression on Alex's face was so worth it.

"I'm kidding, man. I'm kidding. Relax."

Alex handed the cigarette back and sat down next to me. "Hey, who am I to criticize? I'm a vampire."

"I didn't really eat him. I dumped him in the woods. They found his body, assumed he'd been attacked by wild animals, and came to tell me. The autopsy confirmed that there was no other method of death. Like, he wasn't killed and dumped. They decided the lack of blood at the scene was because the animals had dragged him around.

"That's the main reason I moved to the apartment. My room was covered in blood. I cleaned it and painted over it and replaced the carpet, but I could still smell it. I couldn't live like that. What about you? Your parents."

"They're alive. I haven't seen them or contacted them since I got turned, but I looked them up once I left Xyj'Ru. They had me declared dead three years ago. I've got two sisters, a brother-in-law, and a nephew."

We lapsed into silence. There wasn't really anything more to say; at least not on that topic. It was a nice night. Clear, chilly, and sitting there in the park the dominant smells were dirt and plants and small animals like squirrels and rats. There were a few stray cats as well, and somewhere there were ducks. I could smell a pond, so there were probably also fish and turtles.

Alex's shoulder was pressed against mine and he had his eyes closed. His soda cup was clutched in his right hand. I thought he'd fallen asleep. I envied him. For a vampire, he was a pretty normal person. A little immature, but very human.

"Hey, Nicky? I'm Hungry."

I was about to make some sarcastic remark when I realized there was something different about the way he said "hungry." I thought back through all the days and weeks we'd known each other and I couldn't think of any time he'd fed. Not with me knowing about it, at least. Aside from stopping my lip from bleeding, anyhow, which hadn't been a lot of blood, relatively speaking.

I used my limitless mental faculties to process things. "Uh," I said. "We'll talk about this tomorrow." Wise words. Wise words, indeed.

We walked the streets and roamed through the park, but saw

nothing more interesting than hookers and their clients making arrangements. Just before sunrise, we went back to the restaurant to wait for Buck. We saw his replacement go in, then a few minutes later Buck came out. We followed after him like stray dogs might.

We followed the same procedure as we had the day before. This time, after we'd gotten some sleep and Buck had gone to run some errands, I took a long, hot shower. We made use of Buck's washing machine and got ourselves looking somewhat respectable again.

"We should get the car," I said while Alex studied a pile of individual socks and attempted to pair them all. The car was still parked in the lot at the hotel. I assumed it would be safe there.

People going on trips by bus were likely to leave their cars parked there for more than a day or two, but I didn't want to push my luck and find out it had been towed somewhere.

"I should have a real Meal," Alex said. He tossed a balled-up pair of socks at me.

I caught it and put it in my bag. "I don't want to know what this entails, do I?"

Alex shrugged. "Might as well see it. We've got to get the car, anyhow. We could combine the two."

I had complained that I didn't know much about vampires. I was about to get another lesson.

The second we stepped on the bus an assortment of foul smells assaulted me: urine, shit, garbage, sickness, sex, sweat, and the musk of domesticated animals. The sticky-sweet odor of rotting food and the antiseptic stink of industrial disinfectant mixed with the baby powder and candy scent of children. All of this was carried on the common thread of despair. Even the infants had begun to think that this life was nothing but pain. There was not one happy soul anywhere on the bus. Except for Alex. He inhaled the scents and emotions, cherishing them with as much fervor as I rejected them. A delicate cast of pink touched his cheeks and his eyes were bright with this early phase of hunting.

I pitched my voice low so only Alex would hear, although considering the volume of the conversations around us, it might not have been necessary. "Why are we doing this?"

Alex's reply was just as low. "How do you decide what you're going to have for supper?"

"I go to the grocery store."

"Exactly. Think of this as the human equivalent of the lobster tank. Only instead of tapping on the glass to decide which bottom-feeding shit eater you'll take home, you're much closer to your choice.

"Essentially," he said, the faintest hint of a smile playing on his lips, "if you're not Kin you're kibble."

I didn't need to kill for food and I'd never had the desire to kill for sport. Most of my life had been spent passing myself off as a normal human being. This was one thing I hadn't really thought about the whole time Alex had been creeping into my life—how he had dealt with his need for blood. How often he'd needed to feed.

My thoughts were interrupted by Alex's gentle tugging on my

sleeve. "That one," he said. He pointed to a rail-thin woman about to get off the bus. She swayed with the motion of the bus, looking as if her legs would collapse under her at any moment.

We stood behind her, flanking her, although there was no need. She was so high on methadone that anyone could have handled her. Alex had chosen the easiest target: slow, helpless, and likely to not protest or struggle too much or too loudly.

We followed her off the bus. Alex paused and looked around, lighting a cigarette. The other people walked off, went into stores and homes, and our quarry staggered and swayed down the street like a marionette in a child's hands.

Alex quirked an eyebrow at me after he smoked half his cigarette. It was time.

Even at a slow pace, we caught up with her quickly and then got in front of her. As we passed a narrow alley, Alex ducked into it while I stopped to tie my shoe, directly in the woman's path.

The woman stopped and looked down at me as if she couldn't figure out how to walk around me. That gave Alex all the time he needed.

The woman made no sound when Alex grabbed her. The only sound — barely perceptible even to me — was the sound of her sweatshirt tearing as he pulled it away from her throat. I moved closer to the end of the alley, keeping watch. The street contained mostly shops that had closed a few hours (or perhaps years) earlier. Pedestrian traffic was light and cars slid by without any indication the drivers even glanced my way.

I turned and looked in the alley. Alex's back was to me. I could see the woman's face; her head was resting on his shoulder. Something like pleasure had torn through the drug-induced fog and gave a light to her eyes that had probably been gone for years. For an instant she was the beautiful girl she had been before she found drugs.

Alex lowered her to the ground gently, propping her against the wall. She looked like she'd just fallen asleep. Alex crouched next to her for a minute and smoothed her hair away from her face. "The end," he said. "No more addiction. No more pain. No more troubles. More than likely, her family will be glad they don't have to worry about her anymore."

"Don't the drugs affect you at all?"

"A little, yeah." Alex nodded slowly. "It'll burn off much faster, though. You shouldn't let me drive. Just in case. And feeding makes me a little wobbly anyhow. Come on. We can't keep standing here. Someone will remember us."

We walked the rest of the way to the car.

***

Another night passed. In the morning, we went to the Central Pratt Library and started our research into the origin and area of Howler. Alex and I sat side-by-side, hunched over newsprint and microfilm copies of the community's free, weekly paper, reading the crime blotter and "feature" stories, and the cross-referencing them with the state-wide publications. We also pulled video footage from local news broadcasts when we found something that seemed particularly relevant.

Evidence seemed to put his first appearance in the early 1980s. "I forgot how bad the hair was in 1984," Alex said as he skimmed through a disc of nightly news footage. "Always liked the Mod look of the sixties, myself." He looked up and found me staring. "I watch movies! I'm only twenty-three, I swear."

"Thirty-three, with a technicality."

"Technicality, schmecnicality. Give me the list."

I slid the paper over and he marked off several tick boxes. Then he attacked the page with a ruler and a crayon he'd found wedged under the microfiche.

"Wish I had some other colors," he muttered and continued drawing, using hash marks and dots to fill in and shade the graph that was taking shape.

Finally, he leaned back and let out a long breath. "I was a math major. Probability. Statistics. Graphing." He turned his graph so I could see it and explained what it showed.

"See, this is the general region Buck gave us. Operating just in those borders, using the reports you flagged as supernatural, we get this smaller area. I drew boxes to indicate the individual assaults.

"The different patterns in the box indicate the intensity of the encounters. They go from what's probably what you and I felt, to murder."

"What are the question marks?"

"If the same person or people were involved in another altercation on another day. Buck said Howler can only touch you once, so either it wasn't Howler, so it's not part of our pattern and just coincidental, or there was something different about the situation. Like there was a third person the second time, and he's the one that got touched and the other two just got roped into it."

I stared at Alex with something like awe. "You've been holding out on me. And all this time I thought you were an idiot."

Alex smiled almost shyly. "I am an idiot. I'm just quick with numbers."

"No, you did great! This is really useful."

He shrugged. "It's not as good as knowing what the key is for."

I grinned and scratched the back of his head. Alex wiggled like a puppy. "I've got a feeling we'll figure that one out, eventually."

We collected our data. We stopped on the way back to the diner and bought a box of colored pencils and a pad of actual graph paper to make Alex's job easier. He continued to draw his charts and graphs. I felt smug. Satisfied. Cocky.

We were going to beat Howler. Then, flushed with our success, we'd take on Xyj'Ru and defeat him, too. I just knew it.

It was nearly midnight when Alex declared himself "spent" and insisted that his "head would explode" if he graphed any more. I suggested we go out drinking.

We managed to drink quite a lot between midnight and one, and by closing time neither of us was feeling any pain. Our conversation had degraded into slurred jokes and snorting laughter. The fact that we now had two demons to deal with instead of just one was the furthest thing from our minds.

Until Alex pulled his keys from his pocket.

Alex took the key off his ring and spun it on the table. It turned in a quick circle, ending each time with the teeth pointed at me.

Alex picked it up again and made a turning motion. "Maybe it's the key to your heart," he teased.

I snatched the key from his hand and examined it closely. It was heavier than I expected it to be. The wood was dense and as far as I could tell, very old. It was also remarkably clean. He'd been carrying it in his pocket and there wasn't a nick or a scratch on it. It was cool to the touch and didn't seem to be warming in my hand.

"You have no idea what it opens?"

"Not a clue. He kept it on a brass ring and would carry it around with him. He'd spin the whole ring on his finger like some sheriff in a Western."

"You never saw him open anything with it? Never heard him mention what it was for?"

Alex shook his head vehemently. "I thought it was just a good luck charm. I took it because I thought it'd piss him off."

"It worked."

"I mean I thought he'd say something like 'that miserable shit' and forget about it! I didn't think he'd, you know, try to kill me because of it!"

"You spent a decade learning from a demon and never really picked up on the fact that they're ruthless and needlessly savage? Considering that's what he was teaching you to be, I'd think that fact would've sunk in."

"In my defense, time moves differently in the demon realm so I wasn't really aware it was ten years. I mean look at me! I don't look ten years older, do I?"

"Vampire!" I shouted and smacked Alex in the forehead. Fortunately we were the only customers in the bar. "You don't age at all, you idiot," I hissed. "You're never going to look older! You didn't learn anything. You know even less about what you are than I do. You don't know anything about the demon that was keeping you. You don't know anything about anything. I'm surprised you were graduating college!"

Alex slid down in his seat until his chin was level with the table. His knees bumped against mine. "Hand me over to him."

"I should."

"I wish you would! I'm useless. You hate me. You'd rather be alone and miserable, anyhow, so what use am I?"

I stood up, grabbed his collar, and hauled him to his feet. "We're going outside. Right now." I was growling. Alex's eyes moved back and forth across my face, rapidly scanning me.

"Are you... changing?"

"No. I'm just going to kill you." I shook him so hard his teeth clicked.

His eyes darkened and his lips pulled back in a smile that was more like a grimace. I threw an extra ten on the table and we slowly made our way out of the bar while the bartender focused on the television. All the better to not identify you, my dear.

We walked stiffly, my hand gripping his shoulder so tightly that I threw him off-balance. He latched on to my arm. "Nice and slow," I growled. "We're just two drunk guys trying to get home. Don't look at anyone. Don't make eye contact. Don't draw attention to us."

We turned the corner and stood in a narrow alley that angled away from the main street. I shifted my grip and stood Alex in front of me. My thumbs pressed into his throat and he coughed as he struggled to catch his breath.

"Nicky?"

"Howler."

"How? Buck said...."

"Maybe because we're different. Maybe Howler got a rush from shifter blood, too. Remember that? Remember what it was like to taste my blood?"

I backed Alex up against the wall and shoved. His head connected with the rough brick. Something cracked. I hoped it wasn't his skull, but I couldn't stop myself. I pressed against him and pinned him there, much like he'd done to me the first night we met. "You want to taste it again, don't you. You want to open my vein and drink me dry, isn't that right?"

We were standing so close I could taste his breath. I could feel the hair on the back of my neck starting to rise. Alex's hands were scrabbling under my jacket, pulling at my shirt.

Even in the dim light I could see that his eyes were almost entirely pupil. He was in hunter mode, as was I, but he was manipulating the fight in an entirely different direction.

He raked his nails across the small of my back. I jerked forward and smacked him against the wall again. This time I knew I heard something crack.

I forced my hand behind his head and felt something warm and wet. Blood was also welling up in the furrows along my back. "It's not working," he said. Then Alex turned things up a notch.

We kissed. It wasn't a polite sort of kiss, either. It was open-mouthed, lingering, and frantic. My fingers were tangled in his hair. I could feel the blood from the cut on his scalp as it oozed through my fingers. A line of sweat rolled down my back and stung as it passed over the scratches. Alex's hands were in the pockets of my jeans, groping, then he was kneading my back again.

I opened my eyes when warm metal touched my skin. Alex's eyes were open and I could tell by the feel of his mouth against mine that he was grinning. I looked at the hand he held up and out to the side.

An iron pellet trembled in his palm.

"Next time," I said as we straightened our clothes, "tell me if you're going to turn up the sex."

"That wasn't me. If it was another taste of you it wanted, I was just going to draw your blood and then trap it when it went in to feed. You're the one who got all kissy with me."

"Because you coerced me!"

Alex handed me the pellet. "Whatever you say, boss. You hungry? I'm starving."

The Pardoner's Tale

Chapter Five

One month later...

The trouble with a job like ours - mine - is that you don't often get praised for it. You can't exactly call City Hall and say, "Guess what! My friend and I got rid of a demon that was bothering the locals. Can we get some sort of a cash reward for that?" What you'd get is a one way ride to a state-run mental health facility.

It was different when Albert was alive, of course. He had money. He had a successful business dealing antiques to collectors, selling the less-rare things in a shop, and occasionally had people with money hire him to take care of a possession. Albert lived well, paid me well, and was well-off enough that he could do jobs for free. I think he would have done favors for people in need no matter what, because he did what he did because he believed in it.

It was a job I had come to believe in, as well. Though I had to admit that the money in the bank wouldn't hold out forever, and living in Buck's basement wasn't going to work forever, either. For one thing, Alex and I had quickly gotten tired of taking turns sleeping on the floor, and I wasn't too keen on sharing the pull-out bed with Alex. He had a tendency to get a little... personal in his sleep, if you know what I mean.

We were both, however, certain that what we were looking for was in Baltimore. Or at least we hadn't reached the conclusion that it wasn't. So we found a cheap apartment over a strip club. Three hundred dollars a month. Furniture from thrift shops (and there were plenty in the area), mattresses from a discount warehouse, and a television from Wal-Mart.

I was half-heartedly looking into what it would take for me to set up shop as a PI in Maryland. Alex was whole-heartedly wooing several if not all of the strippers in the club downstairs. Three times already I'd spent the night at the Drunken Sailor while Alex "entertained."

We were both taking our drinking quite seriously. Neither of us was taking the search for the lock for Alex's key seriously at all.

Until the morning the police came to our door.

Alex doesn't need to avoid sunlight, but he does tend to sleep very deep during the day. This may or may not have something to do with the fact that we often stayed up drinking until dawn.

I'd done my fair share of drinking the night before, so neither of us was quick to respond to the buzzing of the intercom. Eventually I poked my head out of the window and looked down at our street-level door.

"Company," I said.

Alex peered out from under a pile of blankets and mumbled "Xyj'Ru?"

"Do you really think he'd bother with ringing the bell? It's a cop. Get dressed." I hit the speaker.

"Can I help you?"

"I'm Officer Doderberg. I'm looking for a mister Pardoner or a mister Finch, regarding Charles Whitmore."

"Buck," Alex said as he pulled a tee-shirt over his head.

"Wonder what he's done?"

"I'll buzz you in." I said into the intercom. "Come straight up the stairs to the third floor."

Officer Doderberg appeared to be about seventeen years old until you got a look at his eyes.

Being a cop adds years in a hurry. Especially when you get the sort of job that Doderberg had.

We all sat. Officer Doderberg folded his hands in his lap and looked from me to Alex and back again. "How close were you to Mr. Whitmore?"

"Friendly," I said. "He helped us out when we first got here."

"Have you seen him recently?"

"No," Alex said.

"About a week ago," I said. "What's happened?"

"Where were you last night?"

There was a subtle change in Alex's scent. A little edge of fear. The cop looked curiously at

Alex, almost as if he picked it up, too.

"We were here. Both of us. We were, ah," I glanced around. There were still empty bottles next to the television. "Pretty drunk," I admitted.

"You didn't go out at all?"

"Alex went to the liquor store about six p.m., but that's it."

"And no one else can vouch for you?"

"Will you get to the point?" Alex blurted. The cop and I both looked curiously at him this time.

"The Drunken Sailor was robbed last night. Charles Whitmore was murdered in the process."

I excused myself and went to the bathroom. I vomited twice, thought about the last time the cops showed up to ask me about a murder, and threw up once more for good measure. When I went back to the living room I overheard Alex telling the cop about Albert and Linda. I turned around and went back into the bathroom, but stayed tuned to their conversation.

Officer Doderberg thanked him, handed him a card, and left. Once I heard the street-level door close, I walked over to the sofa and sat.

"You're an asshole."

"What did I do?"

"You told the cop about Albert?"

"Yeah, so? It's not like you killed him."

"Two people I was close to are murdered. The next place I settle, someone dies. Don't forget that my father was murdered, too. That's four people murdered, and me the common point. What's that going to sound like to the police?"

He stared blankly for several long seconds. "Oh," he said. "I see your point. Though to be fair, you did kill your father."

"Alexander."

He raised his hands and leaned away from me. "Calm down, man. I'm sure they're not going to think you were in any way responsible. They said Buck was killed during a robbery. Nothing at all like what happened to Albert and Linda."

The next day, when the story hit the news, we realized how wrong we'd been.

I spent an hour staring at the paper, then went online and checked some of the less reputable sites. Sure enough, the crime scene photos had leaked. There was Buck, on the floor, behind the counter, with his internal organs oozing out of various holes.

The newspaper said the cause of death was blunt force trauma. The officer interviewed said it looked like he'd suffered several sledgehammer blows to the chest and stomach, followed by multiple stab wounds.

The paper said, "We believe Mr. Whitmore tried to stop the robbery. As a result, the perpetrator or perpetrators brutally attacked and killed him."

"Our friend Xyj'Ru," Alex said as he read over my shoulder. He wasn't asking. We both knew it had been. It'd been a demon with sledgehammer-like fists and claws like knives. I was glad that we weren't living in Buck's basement anymore. Not that that would have saved Buck, but it extended our life expectancy by a little bit. A few days. Maybe a week.

"He's tracked us here, Alex. He killed Buck. He knows we're here and he knows we're close and..."

"You don't think the cop..."

"No. No way. We'd be dead already."

"Unless he's lulling us into a false sense of security," Alex said matter-of-factly. "Do we take off again?"

I shook my head. "What's the point? He'll keep following and keep killing people and eventually he'll get bored with the chase and we'll be dead. We might as well stand our ground and take our chances."

"If we're going to die, I just want to say that I'm glad I met you," Alex said.

"I wish I'd never met you," I replied.

***

Thirty-seven hours.

At thirty-seven hours and five minutes, while we were aimlessly wandering the streets of Fell's Point, a very large, very scary looking man approached us and backed us into an alley, where his bigger, scarier friend was waiting.

The arms alone on these guys were intimidating. They looked almost too long for their bodies, giving the men an apelike appearance. The protruding foreheads and the dead, glassy eyes didn't make them look any more human.

The taller of the two glared at me. He drew himself up to his full height and swiveled his neck, warming up before the dance.

"His neck is as big as your bicep," Alex muttered as he readied himself for a fight.

"His bicep is bigger than your waist," I exaggerated and felt around inside me for the wolf. I panted softly, tasting the air. "And they're mortal. Human."

"Xyj'Ru underestimated us." Alex grinned and I caught the change in his smile and his eyes. "At least I hope he did. Think we can take them?"

"We're probably more flexible than they are, what with all the muscles we're lacking. Probably faster, too. Unless Xyj has souped them up demonically."

"Can't tell. You going to... you know?"

"Yeah. Going to be awkward, though. I don't really want to turn my back so I can get undressed." I shifted and wiggled while trying to get my shoes off.

"NickyIreallydon'tthinkyouhavetimeto..." he shouted as the mountains came toward us.

I had one shoe off. I picked it up and threw it at the closer of the two thugs. It smacked his forehead and bounced off to hit the wall. Werewolf, zero. Caveman, one.

I managed to get my other shoe off just as the taller guy lunged at me. Now I ask you... how is this fair? Alex has a good three inches on me at least, and the shorter one takes him on? I threw my other shoe. This one landed right in the middle of the ape man's face. It only made him angrier.

Alex was fully vamped out. I caught a blur of movement out of the corner of my eye and knew it was him, moving with vampiric speed. My opponent (I dubbed him "Frick") took a swing but ended up punching the wall. His fist tore a large chunk out of the bricks and he scattered clay and mortar dust when he pulled his hand back again. I dodged quickly; I knew he wouldn't miss a second time.

I kept looking around for anything that could be a weapon. I threw handfuls of dirt in Frick's face, hoping to blind him at least long enough for me to shift. Hopping around barefoot and flinging silt wasn't going to keep me alive for very long. I needed the wolf.

A bottle! I thanked whatever higher power might be out there (just in case there was one out there) and slashed at the thug's face. I was hoping to take out an eye. I managed to give him a nasty gash across his forehead and cheek instead. Still, I was taking what I could get and I used the few seconds it bought me to start calling up the wolf.

I saw Alex. He was on his guy's back, legs wrapped around Frack's neck, arms flailing in an attempt to punch him in the face. Frack was too strong; he grabbed Alex's legs and threw him against the wall. Alex hit upside-down and landed on his neck on the pavement.

Thinking he was down for the count, Frick and Frack both dove for me. I threw myself on the ground and scrambled between the feet of one of the boys. I was crawling through something foul-smelling and sticky, but the fact that they were having trouble crouching on their over-muscled legs made up for it.

I could have made a break for it. I could have dashed for the end of the alley, took off down the street, gone far, far away from this place. Alex was the one they really wanted. Alex was the one with the key. Alex was the one who betrayed Xyj'Ru.

Alex was also my best friend. There was no way I was leaving him at their mercy. So there, at the mouth of the alley, barely hidden by a shadow, I shifted. My two new playmates got to witness the bone splitting, muscle tearing, clothes ripping, painful, horrible shift.

They *had* underestimated us. I guess Xyj didn't know I wasn't under contract to the moon, so he hadn't warned his henchmen. *Idiot,* I thought. *How have you lived this long? Oh, right. By getting other people to do your dirrrrty worrrrr.* The thoughts became a snarl and humanity was displaced.

I have several fuzzy (furry?) memories of the next series of events. I remember the taste of blood and the sound of tearing flesh. I remember the taste of Alex's skin and hands that felt like Alex's gripping the fur at my neck. I remember the sound of Alex feeding before the corpses got too cold and the smell of blood on his breath. And mine.

I remember herding him home by bumping my head against his thigh and pulling his pant leg to steer him and my fucking tail wagging a mile a minute the whole time.

Eight or ten hours or days later I woke up in Alex's bed, human again. The sheets were caked with blood and garbage. The whole room smelled like rotting things. *We* smelled like rotting things. Alex was pressed against my back, one arm draped over my side. The other was bent beneath his head. His elbow was jabbing me in the back of the neck. I squirmed away and turned over to look at him.

He was a mass of cuts and bruises. Blood matted his hair and streaked his face, neck, chest, and hands. I tried to see myself but lowering my head sent electric jolts of pain up my spine. Inventory could wait. How we'd made it home in this condition was anyone's guess.

"No one saw us," Alex mumbled.

"Huh?"

"You just said 'how'd we get home'. You were a wolf so you looked like a big dog. Anyone who looked at me didn't really see me. It's a vampire thing." He eased himself onto his back, wincing with pain. "I've got some broken ribs, I think."

"I'm surprised your neck's not broken."

"Me, too." He wiggled a little, trying to find a less painful position. "Fuck, do I need a shower.

We both do."

"I'll go first." I slid out of bed and waited a few seconds for the room to stop spinning. "When you're in there I'm going to burn our clothes, and probably these sheets. Maybe even your mattress."

Alex yawned and made another attempt to get comfortable. "I'll just sleep in your bed, then."

***

His hand folded around mine. His leg pressed against mine. My palms started to sweat, and he laughed.

"Not letting go," he said softly.

"Not trying to make you."

"Thought you were trying to sweat me out."

"Nah."

Alex moved to kneel over me, one leg between mine. I leaned back and propped myself up on my elbows. He grinned, licked his lips, and bared his fangs.

"You'll like this," he said. "I promise."

He nuzzled my stomach through my shirt. Every muscle in my body contracted and he laughed again. "I can't believe you're scared." He carefully rolled the hem of my shirt up, exposing my stomach.

"I'm afraid of the foreplay, not the event."

His mouth was hovering over my belly. I could feel his breath when he spoke. "We can skip it. Most people like it, though. It sets things up so it doesn't hurt so much."

"I'm not most people. Let's just skip to the main course, okay?"

He shrugged, licked a small patch of skin, and then bit. His fangs broke through and I felt the rush of blood and endorphins. My arms gave out and I collapsed flat.

Five minutes. That was all. Five minutes, and it was just a surface wound. It was already an ugly purple, but it wasn't bleeding. It didn't even really hurt. Basically, it was a hickey.

Alex swayed and sighed. "That's really good shit." He flopped next to me and put his head on my shoulder. "Was it good for you too, darling?"

"I thought it was going to energize you, not get you drunk!"

"It's not my fault your blood is eighty proof. I'm kidding! It will. I promise it will. Once the initial rush wears off. It's got to work itself into my system, you know? I can feel it working already. My ribs don't hurt as much."

He rolled onto his back and gave a catlike stretch, closed his eyes, and yawned. "Hey, Nick? What's ironwood?"

"It's a kind of tree. They make golf clubs out of it. Why?"

"That's what the key is made out of."

"How'd you find that out?"

Alex shrugged one shoulder – awkward, since he was still on his back. "The other day, when I was out, I showed it to someone who said it looked like ironwood."

"And you just thought to tell me now?"

"I forgot what it was called!"

"Ironwood is not a difficult thing to remember." I sat up again and reached for the computer.

"It's not difficult to forget either." Alex lounged on the floor, staring up at the ceiling.

"No, I guess it's forgettable when your main priority is orgasm."

"Hey!"

"Oh, tell me you weren't trying to score when you found out. All the information in your head got shot out with your come."

"At least I can come. When's the last time you got laid? When's the last time you even jerked off?"

I mumbled, "It's none of your business," and kept staring at the computer.

"You don't, do you? You're so full of self-loathing that you can't even manage a good wank! No wonder you're so uptight." Alex stood. Even without turning around I knew he was giving me a calculating stare. He was sizing me up. "Nicky... are you a virgin?"

"It's none of your fucking business."

"Oh, my God. I was kidding! You are, aren't you?"

"Didn't I just say...?" I stood and turned around to face him.

"Virgin! A real, live virgin over thirty! Can I touch you? Not in a dirty way, of course. Don't want to tarnish your halo." We were circling each other, waiting for an opening.

I made the first move. My fist met his jaw. His head snapped back. When Alex looked at me again, there was something dark in his eyes. There was also something that looked pleased. He punched me and gave me a bloody nose. He laughed.

I hit him again, in the chest this time, and shoved him. He shoved back, forcing me against the wall. His pupils were blown to the point where there was almost no color left. "You can't take me," he hissed, "but I can take you any time I want to."

To prove his point, he thrust against me. I could feel his cock, hard and tight against mine. Then his mouth was hard against mine in an indelicate kiss. His tongue rasped against my lips, trying to get them apart.

I spat in his mouth. "Fuck you," I said when he backed up to wipe his face.

"In your dreams, virgin."

"In yours." I reached down and grabbed him, squeezing hard through his jeans. "This is what you've wanted since the day we met, isn't it?"

"God, you're bad at this," he said. He moved before I had time to react or even be offended. Zipper down, cock out, his hand over mine, guiding me. He touched his lips to mine again, speaking softly, his low voice vibrating through me. "That's a little better. Slow, like that. Now put this finger here and your thumb..." he paused and drew a shallow, shaky breath, "right there. Fuck, yes."

His tongue nudged again. This time I met it and probed his mouth instead. Until I felt the sharpness of his teeth and tasted copper and tin, at least. Alex laughed through his nose and murmured dark words without breaking the kiss. "You want this so much, Nick. You're fucking hard as a rock."

His hands were down my pants, squeezing and stroking in the confined space, and for a moment, I was helpless. "Come on, Nicky. I know what you are. You can't be afraid to fuck me because of the wolf."

His jeans were down past his knees so when I pushed him off me he flailed helplessly for a second before ending up on his back, on the floor.

"Do not ever say that again." I tried not to stare at Alex's erection. It was difficult to look anywhere else, especially while he was stroking it.

"Which part? Fuck? Me? Fuck me, Nick?"

I tackled him. I sat on his legs and grabbed his jaw, forcing him to hold his head still. I slapped him. I could have killed him. I wanted to. But I didn't want to. I just wanted to hurt him. A lot.

My fingers closed around his throat. I slapped him again. He bucked under me and grabbed not for my arms, but for my thighs. He thrust up harder. He didn't waste time; he unbuttoned, unzipped, and wrapped his fist around both our dicks. He pumped hard, fast, the pressure building quickly. Grinding against me put even more pressure and friction on my balls. One of us let out a low howling sound. It might have been me.

"Just. Come. You. Fucking. Jerk." Alex punctuated with a hard, twisting pull. I couldn't even take a deep enough breath to tell him I was trying.

Alex came first. The warm, wet fluid coated his hand, my cock, and triggered my own orgasm. It was embarrassingly short, painful, and probably not impressive by anyone's standards.

We stared at each other, both of us sweaty and panting. Alex was somewhere between pleased and sated. I probably just looked confused, angry, and sore. He reached up and patted my cheek. "Not bad for a first time."

I glared. "Go get cleaned up. I need a drink."

***

We were sitting in the bar, at a table near the men's room talking about our options when the hair on the back of my neck started to rise. Alex gave me an odd look. Whatever I was feeling, he was feeling, too.

"Well good evening, Mister Finch and Mister Pardoner," a man said in a voice too jovial to be real. We both looked up at the person standing beside our table. He looked familiar, but I was having trouble putting a name to the face.

"Good evening, Officer..." Alex started, then blanked. He remembered more than I did. "Doodlebug," he said.

Okay. He didn't remember that much.

The cop almost blushed and tried to scowl. "Doderberg."

"I was close!" Alex smiled brightly and slid across the bench so he was closer to the wall. "Have a seat, officer."

"John," he said. "I'm off-duty, so you can just call me John."

John Doderberg sat down next to Alex. I kicked Alex. Alex jumped. Doderberg looked back and forth. "I'm not interrupting anything, am I?"

"No," said Alex.

I kicked him again. "Yes," I said.

Alex kicked me back. "No, really. You're not."

Alex was smitten. I wished I was telepathic so I could point out that this was not the time to be hitting on anyone, let alone a cop that might think we murdered someone. Especially when I had just murdered someone. Two someones. But I'm not telepathic, so I kicked him again. Hard. He ignored me.

We fell into an awkward silence. I stared at my beer. Doderberg stared at my hands. Alex stared at Doderberg. The waitress came by and took Doderberg's order. She came back with his drink and refills for me and Alex. None of us had spoken yet.

"So," they both said at the same time. Alex grinned and made a small "after you" gesture. Doderberg coughed and started again.

"So, uh, last... last night." He couldn't look at either of us. Alex went white and looked like he was trying to figure out if he could go over the back of the booth. I put my palms flat on the table, ready to push myself up and run if it seemed necessary.

"Last night," he said again, and then glanced up. The panic had to be obvious. His eyes widened and he stammered. "I'm off-duty! I swear I am! This isn't a sting or anything. I'm here unofficially, as a civilian, because there's no way in hell I can tell anyone at work about this."

"You saw what happened?" It looked like Alex's crush was coming to a screeching halt.

"I did." He drank almost half of his beer in one long swallow. "I was coming by your place to talk to you about... about the other day when I told you about your friend. There was something you did," he nodded to Alex, "that made me wonder if you were... different."

Doderberg looked directly at Alex. "When he left the room, there was a change, like you were trying to push something at me. I knew you wanted me to leave, but there was something more than that. When I left, I kind of had a feeling like I was forgetting something. By the time I got back to the station I had forgotten why I'd gone there. But I keep notes. I've got to because it's part of my job. And I saw on my calendar that I was going there and I remembered that what I forgot was that I'd just gone to see you."

I spoke slowly. "Everyone has forgetful moments, John. Nothing to worry about."

He glared at me. "There's forgetting, and there's having your memory fucked with. That's how I knew what he was. I thought maybe you both were. I thought you might have had more to do with your friend's murder than you wanted to admit. I didn't have proof, though. And it didn't make sense. Vampires just don't do that to people, you know?"

Doderberg's volume was creeping up. Alex put a hand on his shoulder and I pushed his beer closer to him. "Keep it down, please?"

"Oh, don't worry. We get vampires in and out of the city all the time. Most people don't believe it, sure, but..." he shrugged. It was close to what Buck had told us.

"So you were coming by last night to... what? Stake us? Ask us to turn you into a bloodsucking creature of the night?"

"Can I do that?" Alex sounded surprised. "Ow! Knock it off, you bastard. I'm going to bruise." John looked at us strangely and shook his head slightly. "I was going to ask you what really happened to your friend. I knew if you weren't behind it, you had an idea of what did it. On my way there I heard the commotion and thought I'd better check it out. See if I needed to call it in. I saw him hit the ground and you change. I saw him get up when he should have been dead. Then I got the hell out of there before I was next."

"Are you going to turn us in?"

"How? 'Hey, this vampire and this shape-shifter killed those two vics that weren't there' isn't going to go over well.

"After I saw you guys leave, I called it in anonymously and left before the responding officers showed up. Word today is some kid called in a phony report. There were no bodies in the alley. Plenty of blood. Big chunks out of the buildings and some dog hair, but no bodies."

"Wolf," I muttered.

"Huh?"

"Wolf. Nicky's a werewolf."

"You really are, aren't you?" Doderberg nodded. "I really saw what I saw."

"Yep," I exhaled slowly and wished the bar wasn't non-smoking. "And a demon killed Buck."

Chapter Six

We took Doderberg back to our place, sat him down with a bottle of wine, and told him the story of Alex's creation, and our teaming up, and why we were in Baltimore, and what really happened to Buck. He was on his second bottle of wine by the time we were finished, and Alex and I had made it through almost three bottles of gin.

"So, what you're telling me," he slurred, "is that you're a werewolf, he's a vampire, you're being stalked by the demon mafia, and I'm either very drunk because this makes sense, or not drunk enough because I'm scared out of my fucking mind."

Alex hiccupped and leaned over until his head was on the arm of the sofa. "Yes," he said as he closed his eyes. "No one can ever be drunk enough."

"That's not what he meant," I said. It sounded like my voice was coming from somewhere else. Did I always mumble like that or just when I was drunk? "He meant he's not drunk enough because you're a werepire and I'm a cop and he's a wolf."

"No, he's a cop, and you're a wolf. A very sexy wolf, might I say." Alex leaned over the other way and put his head in my lap. "And we're all fucking scared."

"And we're all fucking drunk," Doderberg said.

"Three cheers for Doodlebug. The most observant cop!" Alex sloshed booze on my knee when he tried to get the bottle to his mouth. "Pardon me," he said, and moved to suck the gin from my jeans. I pushed him to the floor.

"Guys," I said. "Guys," I repeated, not sure if I'd actually said it out loud the first time. "Ducking frunk or not, we've got to find an ironwood box."

"What do you mean 'we'?" Doderberg said. He blinked slowly and pointed vaguely at himself. "I'm not in this."

Alex grabbed Doderberg's shoe. "You know too much. You're in, or we have to kill you. I'm not kidding. Tell him I'm not kidding, Nicky. I'm not kidding."

"He's kidding." I fished my own bottle out of its nest between sofa cushions and eyed it. There was just enough left to send me to sleep. "My friend here will just fuck with your memory again." I finished off the bottle and let the world fade to black.

***

There are only a few really effective ways to prevent waking up with a hangover. One is to not get so drunk that you get hung over. Clearly, this wasn't something that existed in my world.

Sleeping until it was gone was also not an option in my world.

Not if I was living with a vampire that never got hung over no matter how much he drank, anyhow. He woke me at the crack of three p.m. by sitting on my legs until my feet went numb.

"How are you?" he asked. He was shower-fresh and smelled like coffee and bacon. Something deep in my stomach did a barrel roll and tried to climb up my throat. I didn't answer him.

"Doodlebug's not doing much better," he said and looked over at the door. Doderberg, pale and sweaty, stood with his arms crossed over his stomach, looking less like a cop and more like something we should be putting into an iron pellet. That almost sobered me up. Almost.

Doderberg collapsed onto Alex's bed and looked over at me. "I almost wish you would kill me."

"You didn't..." I gestured at Alex.

"I thought about it. We might need him. Three heads are better than one."

"Two."

"Yours is pretty much useless right now. I made coffee, if either of you think it'll help."

Doderberg and I both groaned. Good to know we were on the same page.

"I went through the trouble of making it. You're drinking it." Alex left, presumably to get the threatened coffee.

"He didn't make it. He went down the street to the coffee place," Doderberg mumbled. He looked like he was trying to suffocate himself with a pillow. "Until about twenty minutes ago, Alex wasn't so bright and perky."

"Jesus. What's his secret?"

Doderberg held out one arm. There was a bruise in the bend of his elbow.

***

The three of us assembled in the living room again, this time with coffee, the computer, and the phone book. We started contacting every antique store and consignment shop we could find in the state of Maryland. Doderberg used his cell phone, Alex used our phone, and I used the computer.

"What if it's not in Maryland?" Doderberg asked.

"What if it was in Albert's shop after all?" Alex added.

I glared at them and kept typing. I wasn't certain, but I had a feeling that any box made of ironwood would do, as long as we had a way of making sure it was sealed shut. Maybe the key was a key in the sense that it stood for something.

If I were a praying man, I'd have prayed that my hunch was right. The tickle at the base of my spine meant we didn't have a lot of time.

We stopped speaking to each other and focused on our task. Alex muttered that we should have started earlier in the day. I reminded him that he was the one who let me sleep until three. Doderberg reminded me that Alex had slept nearly that late. Alex tossed a pen at Doderberg and called him a traitor. I tried not to think too much about what might have gone on while I was unconscious, and tried not to think too much about why I cared if they got a little "personal".

"You're kidding!" Alex exclaimed and waved to get my attention. I turned from the screen and raised an eyebrow. He was grinning like a maniac and scribbling something on his notepad. "In stock? H-how much did you say? Four hundred?"

I crouched down next to Alex. "Ask if they'll take a personal check."

"Will you take a pers- Oh, you heard him. She says yes, that'll be fine." He listened a little longer. "Yes, tomorrow morning at ten. Absolutely! We'll see you then. Okay. G'bye."

I tackled him after he'd hung up. "Tomorrow at ten?"

Alex, not the least bit concerned he was pinned under me, gave me his familiar, sunny smile.

"They'll be closed in about fifteen minutes. We'll never make it in time."

"We might not make it through the night! Where are they?"

"Ellicott City?" Alex tipped his head back and looked at Doderberg. "You know where that is?"

"Yeah, we'd never get there before they closed."

"Can you get us there in the morning?"

Doderberg sighed and flipped open his phone. "I'll call the station and tell them I'm still down with the stomach thing."

Alex burst out laughing. "Nicky, it's fate. The box? Has a wolf on it." I stared at him for a second, and then, impulsively, I kissed him.

That night, Doderberg slept in Alex's bed and Alex slept in mine, wedged between me and the wall. I didn't sleep much. The tickle at the base of my spine had grown to an itch that was working its way up to the back of my neck.

Xyj'Ru was coming for us. Albert, Linda, and Buck were dead. John Doderberg was now part of this and I didn't know if he had any idea that he was likely to die.

We were all likely to die. A demon as old and as powerful as Xyj'Ru wasn't going to go down easy. I didn't think any of us had the knowledge or the skill to handle this. None of us had the experience.

Chapter Seven

We were on the road by nine the next morning. I drove while Doderberg rode shotgun, giving me directions. Alex lounged in the back seat, playing some hand-held video game he'd picked up somewhere. It was comforting to know he was on alert and ready for action.

It took us almost no time at all to get to Ellicott City. The shop was in the historic district, though, and finding it and finding a place to park was trickier. It was just about ten when we found the store.

The clerk, a woman with long, white hair parted in the middle and hanging loose down her back, smiled when we came in. "You're here about the box, aren't you?" I guess we just looked like the sort of people who'd show up at a gift shop at ten in the morning to buy an ironwood box.

"It's hand-made." She put the box on the counter. Sure enough, a baying wolf was carved into the wood. "You're lucky I had this. We don't get many in because they take a long time to make. They can only use naturally fallen wood and it's sometimes hard to find a piece big enough for a box."

It wasn't a very large box, but it was heavy and strong. I opened it and closed it several times, checking to make sure it sealed shut. "If you want to keep anything in there that needs to be protected, you might want to put something along there." She pointed to the hinge. "Something that will stay kind of soft, otherwise it might just flake off."

She gave me a knowing look and a sly smile. "You just might

want to seal the whole thing with a soft wax to keep anything from getting... in."

I handed the box to Doderberg and wrote the check. The woman leaned across the counter and whispered something in Alex's ear. Alex laughed and thanked her.

Outside, he leaned over and whispered in my ear. "She suggested that once we get whatever it is into the box that we cover it in cement and toss it in the ocean."

***

We had lived through the night. We had the box. We had no plan of attack. The only thing we could think to do was wait. Xyj'Ru would come after us himself. He had to. We'd defeated his henchmen and – we hoped – he wouldn't want to waste more of them. Why send a man to do a demon's job, right? After all, he'd killed Buck himself.

Wait. What?

He killed Albert and Linda. He killed Buck. Why had he sent the two goons after me and Alex instead of just finishing us off? Did he want us alive? Did he want Alex alive? Something just wasn't adding up.

Alex and John were in the kitchen playing poker. I asked Alex to join me in the bedroom. He leered at Doderberg and followed me back to the other room.

"Why, Nick, I had no idea," he said as he pretended to unbutton his shirt.

"Shut it, Alex. Something's not right."

The Pardoner's Tale

"Other than the whole demon-wanting-to-kill-us thing?"

"That's just it. Xyj'Ru doesn't want us dead. Or doesn't want *you* dead."

"Huh?"

"Think about it. He killed everyone else, but then sent two human guys after us. I'm nothing to him. I'm disposable. So there must be something about you that's special. There's some reason he doesn't want you dead."

Alex sat down on his bed and thought about it. "Well, I'm under contract, so I guess I wouldn't be much good to him dead."

Everything in my peripheral vision faded into grey. The only thing I could focus on was Alex's face, and in the back of my mind I was forming images of what it would look like when I was finished.

"You mean to tell me that all this time I could have just handed you over to him and gone on my merry way without you? That this running and fear and living like a refugee could have been avoided if you'd just told me the fucking truth?" I hauled him to his feet and then shoved him back down again.

Alex looked up with his mouth hanging open. "I asked you if you thought..."

"You asked me if I thought giving him the key would be enough. You never once mentioned that he'd be happy to get you back!"

"Who wouldn't be happy to get me back?"

I pulled the pack of cigarettes from my shirt pocket and lit one. "I'm really tempted to just turn you over, you know. This is. All.

Your. Fucking. Fault." I punctuated my sentence with jabs of my cigarette. I clenched it in my teeth. I raked my fingers through my hair and pulled at it. I punched the wall. I shouted wordlessly at the ceiling. Through it all, Alex just sat there, looking at me. Looking at me and waiting for me to hit him.

Fuck.

I sat down on the foot of the bed and cradled my head in my hands. I heard Doderberg at the doorway. "You know 'a word in private' works much better when you're not shouting."

"He lied to me," I shouted, not caring who heard. "He put my life in danger. He put *your* life in danger. He is the one responsible for Buck's murder. I should let you arrest him. I should kill him myself."

Doderberg backed up and raised his hands in a defensive gesture. "Whoa. Dude. What did I miss?"

"All of this could have been avoided if he just went home," I said.

"To Xyj'Ru! To be a contract killer! To be his pet vampire!" Alex shoved me. I shoved him back. Doderberg got between us before we started throwing punches.

"Obviously, there's only one thing to do," Doderberg said. "You give Alex back to the demon."

Chapter Eight

Something woke us in the middle of the night, and we knew that it was Xyj. We needed to meet on neutral ground, so we got dressed quickly and headed out into the cold night.

It was three in the morning. The sky was overcast and the streetlights gave off a sickly yellow glow. The street was empty and strangely quiet. The homeless seemed to have disappeared. Even the mockingbird that was usually raising a racket was nowhere around.

We stood in the middle of the public square, facing each other. In his human guise, Xyj'Ru was a small, old man. His hair was grey and thinning, slicked down against his scalp. There were deep wrinkles on his face that nearly hid his eyes.

"I wasn't expecting it to be this easy," Xyj'Ru said. His accent almost sounded Russian. In the way Chekov on Star Trek sounded Russian.

"I wasn't expecting it to be this easy, either." I stood with one hand in my pocket and the other holding the leash that held Alex's wrists behind his back. "If I had known earlier that all you wanted was your property back, we could have ended this weeks ago."

"I'm not surprised he didn't tell you. I think he knows his punishment for running away is going to be severe."

Something smelled like sulfur and burnt flesh. I saw Alex's nostrils flare. It was the only indication that he was afraid. "Well, come on! Give me back my pet so we can go home."

I nudged Alex. He took two steps forward, then I jerked the leash, pulling him back toward me.

"Wait a second. It's customary to get a reward for returning a lost pet."

"So?"

"So? What's my reward?"

Xyj'Ru grew a little taller. His delicate hands widened and the fingers curled into fists. "I let you live."

I pulled Alex until he was against me. "That's not good enough. I need some sort of compensation. I mean, I'm giving up a pretty good servant."

"What good is money if I have your life?"

"Maybe I've got kids? They might like a little something after I'm gone." I had to stall. I had to keep talking. "What if I want to leave it to charity? Maybe I want to afford a really nice funeral. You'd let Alex be a pallbearer, right?"

The wrinkles in his skin stretched out as he got bigger. There wasn't much time left before he got too powerful to handle. I pushed Alex forward and he started running toward Xyj'Ru. Suddenly, his hands were free, reaching up into the air.

It's moments like this that make you appreciate all the time wasted playing football. Alex jumped up, caught the box Doderberg threw, and slammed it down on Xyj'Ru's head. The ironwood weakened him almost immediately, but not before his fist connected with Alex's chest. The sound of bones breaking was audible in the absolute silence.

Doderberg ran from his hiding place and piled on top of Alex, who was on top of the box, which was on top of Xyj'Ru. In another moment I threw myself onto the pile.

"He's getting weaker," Alex wheezed. His breathing sounded wet.

"Keep the box on him. Get him into it."

"How!"

"Fold him! I don't know!"

Arms and legs were everywhere. Beneath us, Xyj'Ru seemed to be melting or collapsing inward. There was shouting. There was shrieking. There was the fully expected unholy screeching as the box enveloped Xyj'Ru.

And almost suddenly there was silence, and three men piled on top of an ironwood box. We untangled ourselves and stood. Alex sagged to the ground while Doderberg and I sealed the box. Strips of wax coated the joint. Heavy duct tape covered that. And then Doderberg hauled out the bucket of cement he'd been hiding with. He pushed the box into the cement, then used a bottle to shove the box under the surface. We congratulated ourselves on a job well done.

"Guys? I think I'm dying."

"This is going to hurt like hell," I warned Alex, then picked him up like a baby. "Get the bucket, John."

Doderberg grabbed the bucket of quick-set cement and followed me back to my apartment.

Aftermath

At my insistence, John Doderberg stuck around another day. I wanted to make sure there wasn't going to be any sort of retribution from Xyj'Ru's underlings. Fortunately they stayed true to form and the sudden loss of their leader meant they turned to infighting and defending their turf against other demon leaders. They were too busy to worry about us. Or maybe they were just glad that we'd sparked a regime change.

The bruising on Alex's torso took less time to fade than the bruises that covered my arms and stomach. Eighty proof, high-octane, werewolf blood sped his recovery time, but the frequent blood loss did nothing for me, except make me an even cheaper drunk. Alex assured me that once I had recovered from his recovery I'd be drinking him under the table again. He was right.

We decided to stay in Baltimore, in that crappy apartment above the strip club. The rent was great, the location was good, and the bartender downstairs pointed me in the direction of a cheap storefront for rent. Alex and I set up an antiques business. Just as a source of income and to make us a little bit more legit.

John Doderberg stuck around, too. He and Alex are-- well, never mind what he and Alex are. I do my best to not think about it. Not that I care. I mean, it's not like I like Alex or anything.

Anyhow, Baltimore should prove to be interesting. The city's got a long history and a violent past. I'm sure there's more than a few things hiding in people's closets (and wardrobes, steamer trunks, old clocks, tea sets, etc.) to keep me busy. I owe at least that much to Albert.

Book Two: Ace of Wands

Morgan Ferdinand

Chapter One

Stakeouts are the most boring part of a private investigator's job. It's worse when you're a paranormal private investigator, since most of what you're looking for probably doesn't even exist. You wouldn't believe how many people have hired me to look for ghosts or poltergeists, and then been disappointed when I told them it was just air in their plumbing making those clanking and moaning sounds, or it was their very alive, very corporeal, teenage son stealing their shit.

Don't misunderstand me. Ghosts and poltergeists *are* real. Demons are real. They're just not as common as some people want to believe. Out of the twenty hauntings I've investigated in the past year, only three have been anything supernatural.

Vampires are also real. Forget what the movies tell you, though. They're not all suave and sexy and continental. Take my partner (*please!*), Alex Finch. Alex is best described as "lanky." He's a little too tall to be "scrawny." He's also loud, clumsy, and has terrible fashion sense.

Not that mine is exactly G.Q., but that just means I know what I'm talking about.

Anyhow. Vampires. Real.

Werewolves are also real. My name is Nicholas Pardoner, and I'm a Were. I'm also a private investigator who deals with the paranormal. It's a sideline to my actual job as an antiques dealer. You wouldn't believe the antiques that you can collect when you tell someone that something is haunted.

And stakeouts are usually boring.

I just wish they'd *stay* boring. I *hate* when they get interesting.

***

Alex threw himself into the passenger seat with a loud sigh and the audible crumpling of a paper bag from the near-by fast food restaurant. "Ace of Wands," he said as he handed me a cheeseburger and dumped the fries in the bag for us to share.

The Ace of Wands started out as just another touchy-feely, New Age-y, crystals and herbal treatment storefront in a depressed strip mall. The window was decorated to the point of twee with prisms and fairies and gnomes and pewter wizards in snow globes filled with sparkly shit.

It *started out* that way. Sure, the front window still looks like a twelve-year-old girl's bedroom, but my sensitive nose sniffed out something sinister going on during their tea-room tarot sessions.

First of all, business was booming. That might not sound like a big deal, but for a neighborhood where even the Salvation Army store couldn't afford to stay open, something was up. This wasn't a job for pay (a fact that Alex kept bringing up); this was what I considered "community service". In Alex's words, I'm "too fucking noble". Mostly, I can't stand bad magic and stray demons getting their filth all over my city. We've got enough problems here without the paranormal fucking things up.

Alex and I had been parked in the lot for three hours. There had been a fairly steady flow of customers for the first two. College kids -- girls mostly -- and housewives. Holdover hippies of both

The Pardoner's Tale

genders. Then at the start of the third hour, the store was empty, ten women of various descriptions went in, and one of the shop girls flipped the sign to "Closed" and locked the door.

"Tuesdays, one p.m. to two p.m.. Exploring our past selves," Alex read from the flier I'd picked up earlier. "Ever wonder if you were someone important in a past life, Nick?"

"I was probably a mass murderer and you're my karmic retribution," I growled around a mouthful of cheeseburger.

"Yeah, I love you, too." Alex took my right hand and licked burger juice and ketchup from my wrist. The hairs on the back of my neck started to tingle.

"Alex," I warned and gave him a sideways glance. He sighed and slouched back against his seat, reaching into the bag for a fistful of fries. "It's not that I don't... It's just that it's not a good time for that. I won't be able to tell what's you and what's coming from there." I nodded toward the store.

"I know. I know. I'm just bored. I can think of a hundred things to do, and somehow sitting in a car with you, watching women shop wasn't anywhere on the list."

"But trying to have sex with me *is* on the list?"

"Spots two through seven, actually." Alex reached for another handful of fries. "Eating is number one."

In Alex's world, eating is *always* number one.

See, there are different kinds of vampires. Some can't eat anything and have to live on blood. Some of the bloodsuckers have to have human blood from living donors, while others can get by on animal blood, or a supply stolen from blood banks. Alex only needs to feed once in a while, and he can go longer between feedings if he takes it from me. Shifter blood is apparently top shelf.

"Speaking of eating and sex with you," he said, and pointed at my wrist with a fry, "I'm going to need to feed soon."

"Soon isn't now," I said, narrowing my eyes in what I hoped was a threatening look. "Call

Doderberg when we get home. I'm sure he's willing to donate a few pints."

"I'm sure he is." Alex let out a dreamy sigh and stared off into space for a few seconds, grinning stupidly. He was trying to make me jealous. It almost worked. Just to be on the safe side, I decided to ignore Alex and fixed my attention on the Ace of Wands again.

There wasn't a sign of life in the store, but the stench of magic was coming off the place like smoke from a fire. Wordlessly, I handed my half-eaten burger to Alex. *Nothing* put a dent in his appetite.

I couldn't pinpoint exactly what was going on. My first impulse was just simple coercion -- tricking the women into spending their cash on crystals and chakra maps or herbal remedies -- but the feeling was too dark.

"Sex magic," Alex said in response to my unspoken question.

"Think so?"

"I'd put money on it if I were a betting man."

"Congratulations!" I said in my best game show announcer voice. "In a past life you were all concubines! Let's have sex."

Alex stared at the shop for several long minutes. "I wonder if there's room in that class for one more."

At five minutes after two, one of the shop girls turned the sign back to "Open" and unlocked the door. Slowly, the ten women filtered out, talking and laughing. Two of them were carrying shopping bags. They didn't *look* like they'd just taken part in an orgy, but what did I know?

One young woman came out alone. She looked tired. Alex and I exchanged glances; Alex slipped out of the car and walked across the parking lot. He kept looking back over his shoulder and walked right into the woman.

I watched them talk, starting with Alex's apology for running into her. She smiled, but flinched away from him, eying him carefully. I could feel Alex using his Vampiric skills to get her to talk. Despite his charm and ability to put people at ease, her body language stayed tense and focused inward. I wondered if he was getting anywhere at all.

After a few minutes, Alex came back to the car. We watched the woman get into her car and drive away slowly.

"Any point in following her?"

"Nah." Alex shook his head. "She doesn't remember anything that happened. Apparently the guy puts them in what he calls a meditative trance and 'guides them into their past'. They're supposed to come out of it feeling pretty good."

"She didn't look like she felt pretty good." I started the car. Alex didn't look like he felt pretty good, either. He'd understated his need to feed; that small amount of exertion to get the woman to talk had clearly taken a lot of out of him.

"I don't think she knows what happened. I got the smell of sex from her, though."

Shit. "We're going to have to get into one of these sessions."

"I was afraid you'd say that." Alex said without the slightest tone of regret in his voice.

***

Alex put in a call to Doderberg as soon as we walked in. John Doderberg is a cop and a friend. He's also Alex's frequent donor and occasional fling. Not that I care. I mean, what's it to me what they get up to in the course of a feeding?
While Alex was on the phone, I collected the dirty laundry. I figured I'd make good use of my time while they took over the apartment. Anyhow, we were almost out of clean things. Alex was wearing one of my shirts and I had on one of his socks (the other was mine).

"No, I understand," Alex said. "There's nothing you can do about it. I'll just see if Nicky's up for a pint." He was grinning at me when he hung up.

"Hate it when you call me that," I muttered as I walked past. "And no. What's wrong with John?"

"Bunch of people are out sick, so he's gotta go in. Mind if I tap you?"

I glared.

"Come oooon," he wheedled. "A little from you will last me longer than a lot from John. The less I have to feed, the less I'll bug you."

I sighed and rolled up my sleeve. "I would so love to believe that."

Alex kissed my cheek and stroked the inside of my arm. Feather-light touches in the bend of my elbow made me shiver. "You love it when I bug you." His thumb caressed the veins. "The vein in the groin is better, you know."

"I don't care if it drips liquid gold. You get the arm or nothing."

"Not even the ones in your neck?" His breath and lips ghosted across my throat.

I closed my eyes and swallowed hard. "Maybe."

Alex took a step back. I opened my eyes and caught him staring skeptically at me. "You don't mean that."

"No, I don't." I lied. I *did* mean it. Well, I'd meant it while he was that close to me, but once his concentration was broken, his coercion wore off quickly.

At least I *think* he was coercing me.

I sat on the sofa and he sat down next to me, curling up so his head was in my lap. He looked up, leering. "Sure you don't want to go for the groin?"

"Alex, I am going to go for *your* groin if you don't knock it off."

"Fine," he said with a huff. He pressed his mouth to the crook of my elbow, exhaling warmth and exuding an aura of pleasure and calm. I leaned my head against the back of the sofa and sighed. Alex's fangs breaking the skin barely made me flinch.

I dozed while he fed.

Ten minutes later, Alex cuddled against my stomach and yawned. I smiled sleepily at him and played with his hair. "We need a plan," I said.

"I thought I could make dinner, maybe we'd watch a movie. I'd get you drunk and try to get you into bed..."

Alex hit the floor with a satisfying thump.

"I meant about the shop!"

"Oh, right." He stood up and rubbed his ass indignantly. As if I'd actually hurt him. "I think we should send John in first and see what happens."

"You don't think they'll take one look at him and know he's a cop?"

"You don't think they'll take one look at you and know you're a werewolf? Or that I'm a vampire?"

"Am I going in there furry or something? People don't look at either one of us and think 'oh, there's an undead creature of the night'! But people *do* look at Doderberg and think 'that guy's a cop'."

"It's the haircut, isn't it? I keep telling him to let it grow out. Do something different with it..." Alex talked with his hands, gesturing to his own (recently trimmed and tidy) hair. "But no, he says the buzz cut is just more efficient. Less time in the shower if he doesn't have to fuss with it."

Alex was babbling. I tipped my head back, stared at the ceiling, and let him work off some of the excess energy he was getting from my blood. "Yeah, it's the haircut," I said when I sensed he'd stopped talking.

"You weren't listening to me."

I lowered my eyes to meet his. "Do I ever?"

"What I *said* was that maybe you and he could go in together. He could be the distraction and you could look around for anything, you know." Alex made another vague gesture. This one meant "strange supernatural things that I'm too stupid to see." Alex raised his eyebrows and looked hopeful. "If they're busy thinking 'oh, shit! A cop!' they might not even notice a shifter poking around."

I had to admit it was a pretty good plan. And if the shop owner *was* actually skilled in any sort of magic, the place might be protected against anything unnatural coming in. Me, though, I was born this way. You can hardly call *that* unnatural, now can you?

I praised Alex for the idea. He beamed and primped. I stood up and grabbed his face in both my hands. Before he could blink, I pulled him to me and kissed him. The little squeak he gave was satisfying. So was the feeling of his tongue against my lips -- prickly soft, like Velcro or fine grain sandpaper, like a cat's tongue nudging against my own. My hands settled on his biceps and I swear he purred a little.

I was almost sorry to end the kiss, but I couldn't have Alex thinking that I actually *like* him or anything. We'd never get any work done.

Chapter Two

Doderberg sat on the sofa with a mug of coffee in one hand and a book about tarot in the other. He frowned at the page. Then he turned the book sideways. "That's... really kinda phallic, don't you think?"

"All the better to perform sex magic with, my dear." Alex sat next to Doderberg, clutching his own mug of coffee. He yawned and stretched, his T-shirt riding up with the action, exposing his stomach. I noticed that Doderberg noticed Alex's stomach and smiled appreciatively. My eye roll went *un*noticed.

It was four in the morning. Doderberg had come over immediately after his shift ended and woken us from our sleep. Yeah, I know. What are a vampire and a werewolf doing sleeping at night? We don't have a lot of choice. To make money, you've got to put up with the daytime world. See, the whole "vampires can't go out in sunlight" thing depends on the *type* of vampire. Alex's sire was of the line that isn't bothered.

Anyhow, we can both go out during the day, and most of the time we have to. And I *like* sleeping.

I stifled a yawn and outlined the plan. "Tomorrow, you and I will go in there and just look around. You'll ask questions about things. I'll poke around and see if I can sniff out anything."

Doderberg raised an eyebrow. "Questions about *things*? Like what?"

"I don't know. Chat up the girls working there. Ask about love potions. Tell them you think your girlfriend's cheating on you or something. Ask to get your aura read or your chakras dusted."

"Or your nob polished," Alex interjected with a leer and a nip to Doderberg's neck.

I growled. "Can we focus, please?"

"*I'm* focused," Doderberg insisted as he shoved Alex to the side. "I'm going to make small talk with the girls and you're going to browse and see what you find. Easy enough."

"What am I doing?"

I looked at Alex. I don't know *why* I expected him to know what was going on. I mean, it was *his* idea. "You're going to wait in the car and we'll contact you if we need you."

"Brilliant plan. I heartily approve. Can we go back to bed now?" Alex stood up and headed out of the room without waiting for an answer.

Doderberg stood and looked at me questioningly.

I gave a noncommittal shrug. "D'you want the sofa, or a bed?"

"Bed. I won't be able to move in the morning if I sleep on that thing." He followed me into the bedroom.

Alex was sprawled face-down on his bed, but looked up when we came in. "Sharesies?"

I stopped. "Did you honestly just say 'sharesies'?"

Doderberg tried not to laugh. He shoved Alex over and climbed onto his narrow bed. Alex threw his arm across Doderberg's stomach and fell asleep almost immediately. Doderberg didn't last much longer.

Me, I lay there for a while, in my own bed, staring at the ceiling.

***

The next day, just after eleven in the morning, Doderberg and I showed up at the Ace of Wands. We came in, laughing and shoving each other, whispering things like "this is silly" and "just go talk to her." Finally, Doderberg stepped up to the counter and cleared his throat. His ears were bright red.

"Hi, uh, I'm looking for, uh..." he started, and then dropped his voice. The nervous glances he kept throwing in my direction worried me a little until I realized that he was faking it -- pretending to look to me for encouragement, and not to keep an eye on me. I poked around and kept giving him "hurry up already" gestures.

His conversation with the girls faded into the background, turning into a buzz punctuated by the giggles of the shop girls. I couldn't hear them over the loud, insistent humming of dark magic. The closer I got to the back room, the louder it got. The stench was also incredible -- it was like burning tar. How it wasn't obvious to everyone was beyond me.

There wasn't a class scheduled. We hadn't seen anyone come in and not leave. I figured the classroom would be empty. I glanced over at Doderberg and made sure he had the clerks' attention and turned the knob. The door was unlocked and I pushed it open slowly, hoping it wasn't the sort that creaked.

The door wasn't even open an inch when I heard it. The deep, intense noise like a generator powering up. The smell of ozone. And then the painful feeling of an electrical discharge. I blacked out.

When I woke up, we were at home. I was in my bed with Alex clinging to me, almost protectively. Doderberg was asleep in Alex's bed. He had the start of a black eye and a nasty looking cut along his forehead.

"One of the girls was wearing a ring that took a nice chunk out of him," Alex murmured. His voice was thick with sleep and his breath was 80-proof. "I was worried."

I grunted. It figured he'd be worried about Doderberg.

"I meant you, asshole." Alex pressed his face against the crook of my neck and inhaled deeply. I could feel his tongue tracing the veins. I shivered and my heart beat just a little faster. Unfortunately, this made my head pound and I made a small, whimpering noise.

Alex laughed, low and growly, and carded his fingers through my hair, tugging a little. "I can take the pain away," he offered. I was aware of his erection. I was also embarrassingly aware of my own. I hated that he had the ability to turn me on. I hated the realization that I was teasing him less and meaning it more. I didn't *want* to like him. I didn't want to *want* him.

But...

But while his nails scratched my scalp and his teeth grazed my throat and his erection practically burned against my thigh, I couldn't deny that I *did* want him. Alex seemed to sense this and rolled me over and pinned me on my back.

His mouth was warm and metallic. *Doderberg's blood?* I wondered. *Or some stranger's?* The wolf stirred inside me, disturbingly possessive. I ignored the feeling; Alex wasn't mine and I certainly wasn't his.

Alex was laughing into the kiss, snorting through his nose. "What's so funny?" I couldn't make eye contact with him. I knew he was laughing at my fumbling attempt to give him a hand job. I couldn't get the angle right or figure out how to stroke him. I was impressed that I even managed to get my hand inside his pants. My wrist and elbow conspired against me and refused to move in the right direction to do anything.

"Nick, will you just *hold still?* Alex arched his back, positioned my hand, and stared down at me, grinning. Then he began thrusting in slow strokes. I couldn't do anything but stare, watching his cock moving like a piston through my fist.

Alex was quiet when he came. Just a gasp that was almost nothing more than a hiccup. He leaned forward and brushed his nose against mine. "Feel any better?"

"No."

"Really? I feel fantastic." He flashed a grin that had too many teeth and then winked. "Can I..." he drawled and ran his index finger down my throat. "Can I blow you?"

"No," I snapped, and started to move him off me.

"You know, I know what you're scared of." Alex repositioned himself slightly and kept me from moving even a little bit. "See? I can control you if you start to get shifty." He was practically purring in my ear now. I stole a glance at Doderberg. He was still deep asleep and snoring softly.

Alex inclined his head toward Doderberg. "He's under sedation.

One of the girls downstairs had some Percocet."

I squirmed under Alex in an attempt to get free. "Great. A cop getting a controlled substance from a stripper. *After...*" I paused and stared up at Alex. "What *did* happen at the store?"

Alex hung his head and let out a sigh. "If I tell you, will you let me get you off?"

"Sure," I said, nodding. "Sure I will. I just won't be able to enjoy it until I know what happened."

Alex fixed me with a look that said he knew I was lying, but he rolled over next to me and propped his head up. "You opened a door. It triggered an alarm. Doderberg charged for you. One of the girls took a swing at him and tore him up pretty good. The owner came out of nowhere, ranting and cursing -- and I mean literally cursing -- in Etruscan. Something about demanding you have an unlucky day and that he hoped you'd get fleas. Which sounds pretty tame, but if you know anything about Etruscans, it's pretty bad."

I stared at him.

"Xyj'Ru worked mostly in Etruscan," he said.

I stared at him some more. "How do you know what he said?" I couldn't imagine Doderberg remembering an Etruscan curse and being able to repeat it to Alex. Especially not something shouted in the middle of confusion and after a pretty nasty blow to the head. "I mean, how did you hear it?"

"I felt the alarm go off. It was this huge discharge of magic. So I started running for the building. I heard him shouting it while John was trying to drag you out of there."

"So they've seen you?"

"I don't know. The girls were screaming and the guy was ranting so I don't know if they really got a good look at me. Not with all the crap stuck to their window, anyhow. I don't think it'd be a good idea for you or John to try to get in there again, though."

"Not during the day, no. Hey, should he be sleeping if he got punched in the head? What if he has a concussion?"

Alex was already distracted by my clothes. "Hmm? Oh, he should be fine. I shared a little blood with him, so he's going to heal up pretty fast. Damn it. I should've gotten you undressed when you were passed out. Are you really going to let me do this?"

"Is that safe?"

"Sucking you off? Well I'm a vampire and you're a virgin, so I think we're in the clear there."

"I meant..." He was already under the covers and nuzzling against my stomach, making it hard -- I mean difficult -- for me to think. "I meant you giving him your blood. Isn't that how it gets passed on?"

"Yeah, but it's more complicated than just a few sips. The whole feeding nearly to death and then the reviving thing has to happen. The worst that can happen is he turns into a Renfield. But considering he's only had my blood this one time and I won't let him blow me, I don't think we need to worry."

Alex's hands were surprisingly gentle and they completely derailed my train of thought. The slow, steady movement was strangely relaxing. I was having trouble keeping my eyes open.

It got worse when the thumb swiping across the head of my dick was replaced by his tongue.

That catlike, sandpapery tongue.

Drugged or not, I didn't want to risk Doderberg waking up during this. I pressed the heel of my hand against my mouth to keep from making any noise. I wanted to laugh. Never in my wildest dreams had I imagined this. Although I'm sure it'd been wank fodder for Alex for months.

Alex *was* laughing. Little puffs of breath through his nose. I would have been offended if I hadn't been on the verge myself. The laugh vibrated against my skin. Alex followed it with a quick swipe of his rough tongue and I groaned softly.

Alex made a quiet moan in response. My stomach clenched and my balls drew up tight. I wanted to make him make that noise again, so I hesitantly reached for him and played with his hair. He made another small noise and I couldn't stop myself. I tried to push him away, tried to get him to back off, but he put his hands on my hips to steady me and stop me from pushing into his mouth. For once I wasn't going to argue with him. He could have complete control. At least as far as *this* was concerned.

When I'd come, he crept up and balanced over me, holding his face very near to mine. His eyes were heavy with sleep but bright with... victory? Glee? Something. He was getting some sort of high from my come; that much was apparent.

"Wanna taste yourself?" He purred, his lips hovering just over mine.

I pushed him over and turned my back to him. Chuckling, he cuddled up behind me, pressing his mouth against the nape of my neck and wrapping one arm around my stomach.

"Hey, Nicky?"

"What?" I grumbled. I didn't even bother correcting him. I know he knows how much I hate being called Nicky.

"Thank you."

"For what?"

Alex hesitated. "For being okay," he said after a few seconds. I think he was trying to thank me for letting him blow me -- for letting him get that close to me -- but neither of us was going to acknowledge that.

"Hey, no problem. I try my best to not die, and so far it's worked."

"Immortal until proven dead," he said and yawned.

"Shut up and go to sleep, Alex."

"Aye-aye, Cap'n!" He grab bed my arm and made me salute for him.

Jerk.

Chapter Three

I woke up because I was cold and being shoved. Alex had apparently stolen all the blankets and decided to kick me between the shoulders. "What are you doing, you jerk? You don't get cold."

Only it wasn't Alex. There was a mummy in the room instead. Blue eyes and a hint of blond hair looked out from the folds of my quilt.

"Doderberg?"

"They got Alex," he said.

"Why did you let me sleep?" I demanded. I climbed out of bed, stripped off my clothes, and fished around for something cleaner to wear.

"I *didn't*. I woke you up as soon as I woke up. I saw the broken window, realized he wasn't here, and then I started shaking you." His face was still red, but I was pretty sure it was anger now and not the beating he'd taken earlier.

"How long?"

"How long?" he echoed.

"How long was I *out*? Christ, you're getting to be as dense as Alex."

"I don't know," he said sullenly and pointed to his bruised face. "I was out longer than you, remember?"

"You know he might be dead already."

John shook his head. "I'd know if he was." But he looked a little sick at the idea, anyhow.

I'd always known there was more to their relationship than just vampire and donor. Not that I cared. Alex was generally a thorn in my side, so I really didn't care what he did with whom. Not even after...

I wasn't even going to think about that. Instead, I sat down on the floor and fished under the bed for my hunting gear.

John sat in the middle of my bed, still wrapped up. I looked up at him. "I need you to do three things. Cover that window with plastic before we die from exposure. Call my landlord and tell him the window's busted. And then you can write stuff down for me."

***

Alex Finch was not surprised to find himself crucified. He was surprised to note that he was only tied in place, his feet were actually touching the ground, and overall it was a fairly pleasant experience.

He couldn't say the same for his captors. All three of them looked like mud in a roughly human shape. They squished when they moved, dripped water and ooze constantly, and they stunk like a sewer.
"Our master will be pleased to know we've captured the vampire," one gurgled. Another nodded emphatically, spraying algae and seawater everywhere.

"You know the sun is coming up, right?" Alex asked as he struggled against the ropes. Sure, it was only rope, but it was wet rope and it was pulling tighter as it dried in the pre-dawn wind.

The talkative one laughed. Or belched. Alex gagged at the sulfur smell and struggled harder.

"We know it's coming up. That's why you're here. We're going to watch you burn."

"Ah," Alex said. "So the first gentle rays of morning sun will touch my fair skin and make me explode into a fireball that will quickly turn into ash, which will then be scattered on the breeze."

The three lumps looked at each other. At least they would have, if they had had eyes.

"No, Mister Bond, I expect you to die," Alex said to himself and sighed. He wasn't going to tell them that it wouldn't do any good. If they knew the sunlight wouldn't kill him, they'd have to find another way and might actually find one that worked. And, Alex thought grimly, they'd have to touch him again. He was already wondering if the stains in his clothes would ever wash out

***

Once I was fully awake, I couldn't miss the stink of magic. No wonder we'd slept through the whole thing. No wonder no one in the neighborhood noticed the window being smashed and people-or-something going in and out of the third floor.

The bedroom was freezing, but at least the wind was getting some of the smell out of the place. I envied Doderberg and his completely normal nose.

We set up camp in the living room. I took samples and scrapings from the window sill and the floor of the bedroom. John dialed the landlord who wasn't pleased at being woken before dawn.

Before dawn.

Shit.

They knew what Alex was.

"The guy from Ace of Wands made us," I said.

Doderberg frowned. "He did this?"

"He called up something that grabbed Alex," I said and indicated the residue I'd found on the floor. "He knows Alex is a vampire and thinks he's going to kill him with sunlight."

Doderberg relaxed. "Then we've got plenty of time to find him."

"What do you think is going to happen when Alex doesn't burst into flames?"

Doderberg checked the time. "Then we've got about fifteen minutes to find him."

To find Alex before the sun rose, I only had one option. I didn't want to do it, but I couldn't see an alternative. I made Doderberg lock himself in the bedroom and told him to wait until it was quiet before he opened the door.

I stripped off my clothes and stood naked in the living room, cautiously nudging the wolf into wakefulness.

Pain. So much pain. I had an idea that being torn apart by wild animals would probably hurt a lot less. Which is really a bad analogy, since I was essentially being torn apart by a wild animal. Only this one was coming out from inside.

Doderberg had to half-carry me down the stairs. Once we were outside, I wanted to go right back in. The scents coming off the street were overwhelming -- bitter, acid, dirty, decay-sweet -- and something like the smell of raw sewage mixed with the scent of Alex. I whined, and Doderberg scratched me behind the ears. Calming, yes, but offensive to my dignity all the same.

I followed him to his car and whined until he put the window down enough for me to get my nose out. I could smell how nervous he was, but couldn't tell if it was worry for Alex or if he was worried about sitting in a car with an agitated wolf.

"We need signals," he said. "So I know when to turn left and right and stuff."

I smacked the dashboard with my left paw, then my right.

Doderberg grinned. "What about straight ahead?"

I looked forward and nodded, whining softly.

"Turn around?"

I looked back over my left side and gave a short, shrill bark that was too loud for the car. I tried to convey a look of apology.

"Great. All set!" Doderberg started the car and pulled out onto the street.

The system worked. I guided Doderberg into the heart of Downtown, where the scent got mixed with too many other things. It wasn't following a clear path. Not one we could drive, anyhow. Not unless John's car could drive straight across the harbor.

The sun was rising and reflecting bright orange in the rear-view mirror. From the car, we could see the light starting to shimmer off the church by Federal Hill.

I barked and shoved Doderberg's shoulder, pointing with my nose. *There! Goddamn it! Over **there**!* I couldn't shift back here, so I could only hope he understood me.

Doderberg gave an excited "yee-haw" and made a hard turn onto Light Street. We would be there in minutes. Hopefully before Alex's captors realized the sun wasn't going to hurt him.

***

From his position on the top of Federal Hill, Alex could see the first pink light of dawn on the horizon. He struggled harder against the ropes and shouted. One of the blobs flicked a hand at him, spattering Alex's face with mud. Alex retched.

The sun rose higher.

Alex continued his struggle. He was pretty sure he could outrun the lumps, but he had to be able to run first.

Alex writhed and screamed, although no sound was coming out. He wanted to put on a good show, but didn't really want to end up with another mouthful of sewage. The three beings squelched and squished and gave the impression that they were watching him carefully, looking for any sign of smoke or fire.

They moved closer, apparently wanting a better look. Alex

squeezed his eyes shut so tight tears leaked out and rolled down his face.

"He's in pain, but not on fire," one of them said.

He was panting, struggling, and somehow managing not to gag from the foul air. Then he went completely still. The trio pressed even closer.

Alex opened his eyes. "Eiquachud," he said, naming the creatures. "You're done now. Go back to the sewers."

The monsters exploded, covering the hilltop (and Alex) with sludge.

Alex whooped and laughed. Now he could just go home, have a shower, maybe make a sandwich.... Except he was still tied there and all his struggling hadn't done a thing to loosen the ropes.

"Shit," he muttered, and then started shouting for help.

***

We could hear Alex shouting as we ran up the steps to the top of the hill. At least he was bellowing in irritation and not shrieking in pain. The deep, wet, rank smell of sewage was stronger than ever and I knew that it was related to the things that took Alex. Based on the intensity of the stink, I was afraid there would be hundreds of them.

There were hundreds of seagulls instead. They wheeled around, low to the ground, landing, hopping, sparring, and squawking as they fought over piles of algae and refuse. Alex was near one edge of the hill, tied to a hastily-assembled cross.

He was filthy, but I couldn't smell his blood. I would have been able to smell if he'd been hurt, even through the stink of whatever that was.

The smell got worse as we got closer to Alex. Doderberg choked and spat, looking desperate to keep from puking. He managed to cut through the stiff ropes holding Alex. Alex fell to his knees, arms hanging limply at his sides.

"Son of a motherfucking *bitch*," Alex shouted, writing in sudden pain. John and I both moved toward him while his arms flailed.

"Alex!" John grabbed for Alex's shoulders.

"Pins and needles," Alex hissed through clenched teeth. "God fucking damn."

Doderberg sat down on the wet ground and pressed his forehead against Alex's, not caring about the slime. "You scared the shit out of me."

I gave a barking cough before they could start with the eye-gazing and hand-holding. The stench was getting unbearable and I really wanted to go home and be human again. Doderberg at least had the decency to look embarrassed.

"I don't think we would've found you if he hadn't shifted," he said. "He sniffed you out."

Alex threw his arms around me, pressed his face against the scruff of my neck, and spoke so quietly I knew John couldn't hear him. "You shifted for me? I knew you loved me."

I shook until he let go, laughing. "Never show Nicky affection. It makes him grumpy."

I bared my fangs. Doderberg reminded him that being called Nicky also makes me grumpy.

John left us on top of the hill. He needed to go home, shower, change, and get to work. Or so he said. I think he just didn't want Alex leaving demon slime all over the car. Alex nattered on about something as we walked home. Some of it I didn't understand because the wolf part of my brain wouldn't process it. The rest I just chose to ignore. Alex didn't seem to mind.

Alex stashed his ruined clothes in a plastic bag to be dealt with later, then headed for the bathroom. I took the opportunity to shift back, then wiped off as much muck as I could until it was my turn to shower. Do I need to point out that standing naked in my kitchen was enough to make me incredibly uncomfortable? Because it was. I could only hope Alex would be quick.

Ten minutes later Alex was still in there, so I pounded on the door. "You're going to use up all the hot water!"

"Get in here then."

"Fuck off."

Alex opened the door and leered. He was naked, of course, with water clinging to his skin and dripping from his dark hair. Steam billowed from around the shower curtain. "That an offer?" He leered and then shook his head. "Seriously, come in. I'll behave, I swear."

I eyed him suspiciously and tried not to think about what had happened earlier, which only made me think about it. My cock twitched. Alex's eyes flicked down and then back up again. He grinned crookedly and raised one eyebrow.

I pushed past him and made an attempt to shut the door between us, but Alex was faster. He leaned against the door and rolled his eyes. "*I said* I would behave. Just trust me. Get in the tub."

I stepped in and stood under the water. My whole body ached from shifting. Alex stood behind me. I tensed briefly when I felt his hands on me, but I relaxed as he started to massage my neck and shoulders.

"What happened?" I asked and leaned back into his hands, encouraging him to press harder. A knot under my left shoulder blade crunched audibly.

"The guy from the store summoned up three demons. They knocked us out, took me, and thought they were going to toast me when the sun came up. Of course I didn't burn, so they kept creeping toward me to see what was going on. Eventually they got close enough to me that I could hear their name. Then I just had to speak it, get control over them, and send them home. Okay, I *thought* it would send them home, but they exploded all over me."

I looked over my shoulder and glared. "You knew their name?"

"Not at first. Like I said, they had to get close enough to me that I could hear it."

"How long have you been able to do that?"

"I learned it from Xyj-ru."

"And you never thought to mention it?"

Alex shrugged and moved further down my spine. "It never

came up."

I turned around and caught his wrists to keep him from putting his hands anywhere else. "We spend months tracking down and *capturing* demons, and you can just name them and command them?"

"It doesn't work on *all* demons, Nick. Just the ones summoned for a cause. If it's free-range or attached to something, then your way is the only way. These guys were hired thugs. I just took over their contract." He stared at me and grinned broadly, showing too many teeth. He rotated his wrists and clasped my hands. "You shifted to save me." Alex was beyond pleased. He kissed me.

I didn't stop him. I wrapped one arm around his shoulders and put the other hand flat against the wall to hold myself up. The tub was slippery, my whole body ached, and Alex's hands were taking a quick survey of my skin. This wasn't going to work. One of us was going down, and *not* like earlier.

Turns out it was me. Alex's groping led him to my cock and after several minutes my knees gave out. Alex flailed wildly to try to catch me and ended up head butting me in the nose. I sat down hard and let the shower wash the blood off my face.

"I'm starting to think the gods are conspiring against us," he said with a laugh. He perched on the edge of the tub and wriggled his toes in the pooling water.

I pressed the back of my hand against my nose and sighed. "Let's just go to bed. Get some sleep and then figure out how to get into this guy's house and figure out a way to stop him."

The fact that I meant "we'll both sleep in my bed" was

understood. Alex took his favorite spot between me and the wall and pressed his back against mine.

Chapter Four

Ace's real name was Terry Lee Burkart and according to the Department of Motor Vehicles, he was forty-eight. He lived in a single-level house on the shore of a river that smelled faintly like sewage. I suppose that's where his demon troops had originally come from. The road was wide enough for two cars but there were no lane markings. Alex and I watched several cars nearly engage in a battle of chicken until the drivers realized they could actually pass each other with room to spare. Once we were sure the coast was clear, we let ourselves into the house.

The house was small to begin with and made smaller by the books and DVD cases that were stacked everywhere. Most of the DVDs were porn. Some of them were horror movies. The books were almost entirely cheap horror.

"Be careful not to make it look like we tossed the place," I said to Alex as we sifted through Ace's things. Alex gave a snorting laugh and pointed out that the only way Ace would know someone had been in his house was if we cleaned things up.

The kitchen was full of fast food and delivery trash: pizza boxes, Chinese containers, crumpled bags with smears of ketchup on them. Flies buzzed around an overstuffed trash can. There was a stack of blue plastic bags filled with beer and soda cans. At least he recycled. Sort of.

There were more books, more carryout trash, and more porn in the bedroom. Blonde women with obviously fake breasts stared vacantly from the covers of magazines and DVDs. The books in here, however, were allegedly books of magic. Most of them were from Beagmhaitheasach Press, a line his store carried. Alex and I exchanged a look and a grin. "Beagmhaitheasach" means "worthless," and after flipping through three of the books, I could say that they certainly were that.

Under the mattress was the real find. There was several thousand in cash (Alex later informed me it was five thousand, three hundred twelve dollars), and a small book bound in brown leather. It was smooth and warm to the touch and smelled a little meaty. Startled, I dropped it onto the bed and stared at it for a few seconds before picking it up again.

Alex raised an eyebrow questioningly.

"It's made of human skin."

"Ew," he said, and returned to skimming through the collection of porno magazines.

The book explained in detail the steps needed to not only create the mud creatures that had abducted Alex, but also the necessary information to create sex slaves. The handwritten notes stuck in between the pages listed Ace's modifications to the spells: contemporary names to replace the archaic, substitutions that seemed to work well enough (in the absence of the gizzard of an iguana, the bladder of a seagull would suffice), and notes on things that did not work at all.

There was apparently nothing as effective as human blood. I wondered how much of his own blood he'd poured into the incense that was controlling his clientele.

We eventually found the incense and some of the other harder to obtain ingredients. We bagged those up to take with us, as well as the meat book and a notebook Ace had been keeping. The less chance there was for him to reproduce these spells, the better.

Something was bothering me, though. I looked around the room again and rubbed the back of my neck. "I've got a bad feeling."

Alex said, "It's probably just Etruscan fleas."

"No, really. We've got this book. We've got his magic stuff. We've got notes. What's missing?"

"Tongue of wolf?" He leered; apparently the over-abundance of skin mags had given him ideas.

"His room at the store had an alarm on it. Why would he leave the good stuff in his house completely unprotected?"

Alex's grin faded and his brow furrowed. "You thinking trap?"

"I'm thinking now would be a good time to get out of here and lock this shit up. Then we can start worrying about what we're missing."

***

There's a fireproof safe in our living room. It's lead-lined, cast iron, and watertight. It's got a tablecloth thrown over it and a lamp on top to disguise what it is. It's also got a few spells on it to help keep what goes in from getting out. They also help keep anyone who isn't us from getting in.

Alex locked the stolen objects away and then washed his hands repeatedly at the kitchen sink. The feel of the meat book was hard to get rid of. "You know," he shouted over the running water, "he knows where we live already. There's no way he won't know it was us who stole his stuff."

"I know. That's what worries me. He left it out practically in the open. Like we were supposed to take it."

"Maybe he's not really in control. Maybe he wants help stopping what he started."

"You're such an optimist, Alex."

We leaned against the counter, our shoulders touching, and shared a cigarette and a beer. Our fingers brushed together as we passed them back and forth. I felt strangely calm, like a lot of the static in my head was being filtered out. All I could think about was Alex: Alex's dick in my hand, mine in his mouth. What it would be like to just give in and fuck him, knowing that he probably was one of the only people who'd be able to control me if things turned wolfy.

Alex gave me a rueful smile that snapped me out of my daydream. "It isn't me," he said. "I'm not making you think about that. It's not you, either. We handled a lot of stuff charged with sexual energy and it's obviously rubbed off on us. In a manner of speaking." He acknowledged the double entendre.

"Then how did you know what I was thinking?"

He cocked an eyebrow and inclined his head. Oh. Right. The raging hard-on. I crossed my legs and leaned away from Alex, trying casually to hide it, but only looking awkward.

"You don't like me like that," he said and lit another cigarette.

"I'm fine with that. As long as I don't get on your nerves too much with my flirting, it's cool. I mean, it's obvious. Every time I get close to you, you change the subject, find something else that needs to be done, fall down, start a fight, or have a breakthrough."

He squinted at me through a cloud of smoke and passed me the cigarette. "Maybe we *should* go fool around. Might give us the break we need with Ace."

"Maybe I do like you like that. We can talk about it later." I stubbed the cigarette out in the sink. "I think we should go check out the store again."

"Hey, look at that. We only had to *think* about fooling around and you had a breakthrough!"

Chapter Five

It was nearly midnight when we made it back to Ace of Wands. All the lights were off, including the red glow from the alarm system. The front door was unlocked. We looked at each other. Alex was grinning hopefully, sure this meant everything was fine and we were there to play the heroes.

Yep. Alexander Finch: vampire and hopeless optimist.

I wished for my gun. I hated using it. I didn't even like owning it, but it's saved my ass in the past and I was really feeling like it could save it again tonight. This was all shaping up too easily and I didn't like that at all.

Alex opened the door a crack. He reached in and put his hands over the bells hanging from the top of the frame, then slipped in through the narrow opening. If the alarm system was on he wasn't likely to set it off. If it was a heat sensor, it wouldn't find him. If it was a motion sensor, he could make sure it didn't sense him moving. He was standing next to the panel in a fraction of a second.

"It says 'Disarmed'," he confirmed. "Smell anything?"

"Just potpourri and essential oils. And someone's lunch in the trash can." I grabbed the bells and squeezed in, letting the door close completely before I released the chimes. Gently. If Ace knew we were coming -- if he knew we were here -- he hadn't made himself known yet. I didn't want to do anything to rush our standoff until I knew exactly what we were getting into.

Slowly, carefully, we made our way around the shop, looking at things, checking idols and incense and packs of Tarot cards. I ran my hand through a bowl of semi-precious stones and put several in my pocket. I also picked up a tiny, brass bell.

"Ooh, tuna fish!" Alex said happily. "Oh. It's got relish on it." I heard the sandwich fall back into the trash can and shook my head. It wasn't even worth commenting on.

"Start toward the classroom," I said. I felt like I was shouting, but I was barely vocalizing. From the corner of my eye I saw Alex move forward. He was just a shadow. I couldn't even hear his feet on the ground.

"Okay," he said. "It's okay."

I moved much slower than Alex and drew up behind him. "He's in there."

Alex gave a tight nod. "I can feel his heart beating. It's too fast."

"He's scared." I sniffed gently. "You might be right."

"He's lost control?"

"He never *had* control. A demon's been riding him." I could smell it on him.

"What now?"

"Name the demon."

"I can't."

I glared. "You can."

"This is different. Ace *summoned* the demon, but the demon's not under his control any more. That means I can't *take* control."

"Fucking loopholes."

"Don't suppose you have any iron pellets on you?"

"No, I don't have any more, I don't think." I patted myself down to be certain and felt something clinking in my pocket. Frowning, I pulled out the stones I'd pocketed and looked at them.

And grinned.

Hematite!

It wasn't *perfect*. Hematite is brittle and would probably break if the demon got a little too aggressive -- especially since they weren't hollow -- but they would do until we could get home. I made a mental note to find someone who could make me more hollow iron pellets and secured one of the stones in my fist.

Alex kicked in the door and burst through, shouting like he was leading in an entire SWAT team.

Ace was flat on his back in the middle of the room, in the middle of a salt circle. His hands and feet were tied to hooks that had been sunk into the floor. He was naked, sweating, and obviously terrified. He was also out of shape, balding, and scrawny. For his sake, I hoped his dick had shrunk from fear and it wasn't like that all the time.

There were candles everywhere, flickering, casting strange shadows, and raising the temperature to an almost uncomfortable level. I couldn't see anything else in the room, but the smell and the way the hair was rising on the back of my neck was evidence enough. Alex looked like he wanted to sweat. His eyes flicked around the room from corner to corner, never settling on any one thing.

Glyphs in blood and shit covered the walls. A binding spell.

"You have to help me!" Ace sobbed. "He wants my body."

Alex cocked an eyebrow. "Really?"

I smacked the back of his head. "As a host." I looked at the man. "That's it, isn't it? He's been working through you and now he wants to move in permanently. Push your soul out and move himself in."

Ace sobbed harder and thrashed against the ropes holding him in place.

I looked around the room and shouted. "We're not going without a fight, so if you want to pick up your new ride, you might as well show yourself and get us out of your way."

Alex flew backward out of the room and smacked against the hallway wall. He scrabbled to his feet and charged back in. "Habbotep!" He bellowed, jabbing a finger toward the ceiling. "Habbotep! You are commanded to show yourself right now!"

"Habbotep? Seriously?"

Alex gave me a look that said "hey, I don't name them" and shouted to the still-invisible demon. "We're not playing. I name you, and I demand that you appear!"

"I thought you said it wouldn't work."

"I can't control him, but I can challenge him. Get ready to fight."

Habbotep did appear. He was just a mass of sticky black smoke that churned and whirled and stunk. If that was his "corporeal" form it was no wonder he was looking for a human body.

Something made a connection in my brain and I realized that the meat book *was* his body. Habbotep had sacrificed himself to make the book, and our old pal Ace had, by using the book, released him.

Habbotep's form had extinguished all the candles and filled the room with an impossible darkness. I *knew* Alex was standing next to me. I could feel his arm brush against me when he moved, but I couldn't see him at all. I couldn't see Ace. I couldn't see the three hematite stones in the palm of my hand.

It was like a thunderstorm taking place in a twelve-by-twelve room. The air was thick, charged with electricity and the pressure was making my head throb. I expected it to actually start raining. Alex shouted something I couldn't quite understand and some brightness crept in.

Habbotep's form was starting to dissipate. I had to move fast before he disappeared again.

I've used the demon trapping spell so many times I can recite it in my sleep (and probably have).

I held the three stones in my cupped palms and felt them grow heavier as I recited the words. Habbotep was being torn apart and stored in all three rocks.

The pressure in my head was letting up. The room was getting brighter. Alex faded back into sight. He was panting and shaking just a little bit, eyes wide, watching the stones draw Habbotep in.

"Ace," he murmured, and took two easy paces further into the room and knelt to untie the poor guy.

I put the three stones into different pockets. I wasn't sure how long they'd hold him, but at least with him divided, it would take a little longer for him to cause trouble.

Alex helped Ace into a sitting position. I found Ace's clothes heaped up in a corner and handed them to him.

"I don't know how to thank you," he rasped. "You saved my life. I can't ever pay you back for that."

I thought about the money we'd taken. "You already did."

He looked at me. Blond hair lank and stuck to his sweaty forehead, gaunt features and skin almost the same washed out gray as his eyes. There was a flicker of understanding. "You've been to my place," he said.

"Yep."

"So you got the book?"

"And your notes."

"Thank God."

Aftermath

After Ace -- Terry -- had a chance to clean up a little, we took him to a twenty-four-hour restaurant. Two cheeseburgers and a large coffee later, he perked up and was willing to talk.

He'd gotten the book from some anonymous donor. Someone had sent a lot of trinkets and things to the store and included a note that he could use or sell any of it as he wanted. The book was too weird to keep in the store. The shop girls complained about it and customers were afraid of it.

Once he got the book home and started reading it he realized what he had. "It was talking to me when I was asleep," he said, shivering a little. "It told me that if I did what was written on the pages I could have money and power. It was great for a little while. It was great having a store that wasn't failing and being able to pay my bills and pay off some loans. Then the book told me about the women.

"I never had much luck with women." Terry laughed dryly. "Figured if I couldn't get them on my own, why not use a little magic? Only that's when the demon started getting stronger. Started with occasionally having sex with a customer and then it wanted more and more. I was holding those classes, organizing orgies... anything to keep the demon fed."

He looked miserable. Alex got up to find the waitress. I studied Terry carefully. "And that wasn't enough because he wanted to feel it not just feed off it?"

"I might have been able to hold him off, but then you came in and I think he knew his days were numbered. He had to take me over before you could stop him."

I grinned. "We're just a little faster."

Alex returned with the waitress who topped off our coffees. Terry raised his in a toast. "Thank God for that."

Terry pulled a Tarot deck out of his coat pocket. He pulled out the ace of wands, turned it so it was facing me, and slid it across the table. "I chose this because I thought it would be good for business. It stands for new projects and innovation and success." He turned it so it was reversed. "But it all ended in tears. Just like the card says." He sighed, picked the card up, and slid it back into the deck.

"You know your business is probably going to drop off now."

"Can't do worse than an antiques store," Alex mumbled into his coffee. I kicked him.

Terry gave a weak smile, looked at the deck, and held it out to Alex. "Pick two. Just two cards from anywhere in the stack."

Skeptically, Alex drew two cards and put them face down on the table and watched as Terry turned over the first.

"Death," said Terry, "isn't a bad thing. It just means change. Transforming from one state into another."

"Yeah," I said and stirred a packet of sugar into my too-bitter coffee. "I think we both know a thing or two about that."

Terry turned over the second card. "The Lovers. Kindred souls. A partnership."

Under the table, I wrapped my fingers around Alex's. "I think we know a thing or two about that, too."

Short Stories

Death

Contrary to what the media wants to portray, Death is neither large nor terrifying. Death doesn't have a deep, bowel-emptying voice, either. Death is also not a perky little Goth girl.

Death looks more like an accountant of vaguely Indian descent. He stands just slightly over five feet tall and weighs maybe a hundred fifteen. He has soft, brown eyes, small, delicate hands, and black hair with a bald spot so large it looks like he has a Friar Tuck haircut. His voice is so quiet you can barely hear him.

So that's not how people imagine death, but that's what it is. He's just this little guy who checks your paperwork and stamps it either "accept" or "reject." He doesn't kill you; he just makes sure it's your time to go.

Also, Death cannot hold his liquor.

Death was ripping drunk, half-sprawled across the bar, his watering eyes not fixed on anything. I would've cut off any other patron hours before they got to this point, but it wasn't like Death was going to destroy his liver or get behind the wheel and kill someone. Well. You know what I mean.

"It's the stress of the job," he cried for the nth time that hour. "All the people, begging for more time. The weeping family members!" He blew his nose and tapped his empty glass on the bar. I poured him another. "What's worse are the ones who *want* to go, but it isn't their time. I can't take them. They yell. Sometimes they hit me." He blew his nose again and downed the shot I'd poured.

I glanced up at the clock; almost seven. Time to switch from dive bar to *sleazy* dive bar with strippers. I picked up Death's glass. "You gotta go, Dee."

"Yeah, I know." He stood up and wobbled as he pulled out his wallet. "Got a kid in the ICU who's lasted two hours longer than he should've." He dropped a fifty and three twenties on the bar and vanished. I double-checked his tab; he stiffed me on the tip.

Zombies!

So last week we were sitting in the bar downstairs. I was having a drink and Alex was drinking and watching the "cabaret show" on the stage. It's pretty tame stuff by most standards — topless only, nipples covered, no touching, and only a minimum amount of dollar bills being stuffed into G-strings going on. Since we live upstairs Alex and I get special treatment.

No, not that sort. I mean free rail drinks and a steep discount on anything fancy. In return, we keep an eye on the girls when they're coming and going and help get rid of any guy who gets a little too handsy.

Not that we're in there every night or anything. I mean, we live right upstairs so any sort of commotion gets our attention. And if we happen to be out, the bartenders have my number.

Anyhow, we were there and like I said, Alex was watching the stage when he said "Do zombies really eat brains?"

"Sometimes, yeah," I said. "They eat any of the internal organs except the pancreas."

"Really? How come?"

I shrugged even though he wasn't looking at me. "I hear it's bitter."

"Oh you *hear* it's bitter." He looked sideways and grinned at me. I scowled back.

The Pardoner's Tale

Alex turned in his seat and signaled the bartender for another beer. "Anyhow, I was asking because I think there's one right up near the stage."

I scanned the audience and yeah, there was something "not quite right" about one of the patrons. I mean, you expect a little brain-dead, glassy-eyed stare and some drooling when a redhead in a 1970's style roller disco get-up is doing a bouncy little dance, but one guy in particular was a little more brain-dead and drooling than the rest.

"Don't make a mess," the bartender warned as I slid from my seat. Alex laughed softly into his beer.

I gave Alex another glare. "No, no. It's just one Shuffler. I can handle it. Don't worry your pretty little head about it."

"I'll do my best not to fret," Alex said and turned again to watch the show — only this time the show was me, and not Disco Diva Dynette (Sadly, Dynette is not a stage name).

I walked calmly to the guy. He smelled (at least to me) like rotting garbage. Maybe no one else had noticed. Maybe he just blended in with the rest of the guys. I put one hand on his back, just between his shoulders. No heartbeat. No breathing. Just that vacant stare, the drooling, and a nearly constant, low moan of Hhhhuuuuuuuuurrrrr. Classy.

"Sir," I said as I slipped my hands under his arms and lifted gently (You got to be careful. Some zombies are fragile and people tend to get upset if you seemingly rip someone's arm off for no reason), "I'm sorry but your credit card has been declined. We'll have to ask you to leave now."

"Hhhhuuuuuuuuurrrrr."

"Yes, sir. I can certainly call you a cab."

"Hhhhuuuuuuuuurrrrr."

"Absolutely." I steered the zombie back toward the door.

Outside, an off-duty cop who worked the door on Friday nights gave me a look. I shook my head. "Just drunk," I said. "Gonna get him into a cab." The cop muttered an "all right" and I led my new friend Herman around the corner and then to the alley behind the bar.

I turned the zombie so he was facing the wall. I really can't stand shooting something so relatively harmless, but you can't just let the dead wander around like that. It's a health hazard, for one thing. I mean they really are dead. It's also psychologically disturbing to wake up and find the reanimated corpse of a dearly departed sitting on your steps.

Plus, you know, given a chance, they can go all cannibalistic.

Anyhow, it's difficult to put a bullet in something that was human once — and might even still look human — when it's not actively trying to eviscerate you. But I did it. Two bullets: one where the skull and spine come together, and another right at the tailbone.

Fortunately magically constructed things are largely self-cleaning upon destruction. I leaned against the opposite wall and had a cigarette while the body rapidly decomposed. Once there were only a few bones left I carefully collected the bullets and went back to civilization.

Origin Story

May, 1991

I've been cutting pages out of my Moleskine. I'm not supposed to do that. It's not a law or anything. It's just a promise I made to myself. I promised I'd be honest in this book and not censor things, but sometimes what ends up on the pages has to come out.

So since I cut out everything from March to now, I guess I'll start over.

My name is Nicholas Powell. I'm 16. When I was 13 I started being a werewolf. I didn't ask for it. I wasn't bitten. I guess I was born like this. I can't ask my mom because she she died when I was three. I was always to afraid to ask my dad, and now he's dead, too. He died last week.

I think I killed him.

2007

I was thirteen the first time.

Actually, it was about a month after my thirteenth birthday and I was alone in my room, sulking in a wash of barely-teenage hormones. My father had said or done something that pissed me off, so I stormed off and slammed my door. I probably said "I hate you" or some other overly-dramatic thing.

I remember standing there, all clenched fists and frustrated energy, wondering what to do. I wasn't *that* angry, so throwing or hitting things seemed a little excessive. Crying seemed "unmanly." But there was *something* eating at me. Something in the pit of my stomach that was expanding and contracting. There was a buzzing in my ears, pain behind my eyes, and this feeling that something was suddenly very, very wrong.

I can still remember wanting to scream. I can still remember every ache and spasm. I can still remember the utter disgust of pissing and shitting myself as things twisted inside me. I remember vomiting my dinner. To this day, I still can't eat Spagetti-Os.

I stripped naked and crawled into my closet, burying myself in dirty laundry. I stayed there for six hours until the spasms stopped and I could breathe again.

Humiliated, I cleaned up. I did my laundry. I scrubbed the carpet in my room. I cried in the shower.

The next Saturday I got on a bus and went to a library in another neighborhood so I wouldn't run into anyone I knew. I read several books about puberty and realized that none of them talked about what I'd gone through. It would be almost a year before I realized the episodes were tied to the full moon. I would be sixteen before I fully transformed.

When it starts, it's kind of like poison ivy. It's a burning, crawling feeling. It moves quickly to an intense heat and something that feels like millions of tiny bugs poking into your skin. That's the hair pushing out.

It's coupled with a deep bone ache. If you've ever broken a bone and needed to have rebroken to be set properly, it's like that. That's what's happening, basically – your skeleton has to rebuild itself. Muscles and tendons are pulling bone into new places, changing your posture, the angle of your neck, the size and placement of your internal organs... it all has to go somewhere different. You can't scream when it happens. It doesn't take long for you to stop breathing while things move around, and by the time you *can* breathe again, your vocal cords are wrong for it.

I don't know how long it takes. Alex says it's anywhere from ten minutes to almost 45. I think it depends on how willing I am to do it. Fighting against it drags it out and it hurts so much more when I come out of it. I don't fight it unless I absolutely have to.

I stay that way for four hours at least. At least, it's never been less than that. Normally it's closer to six.

I'm sometimes aware of what's going on. It seems like when I do it willingly I retain some... intelligence? Humanity? I have memories from these shifts and I can communicate in a limited way. Basically, I end up more like a very large, very scary dog and less like a wild animal.

When I fight it, it can get ugly. I'm a stereotypical horror movie monster. I have no control. No memories. Alex says that he's almost afraid of me like this, but we both know that it would still be easy for him to kill me. He's the only person that *can* overpower me when the wolf is out. It's one of the reasons why I keep him around. Although the fact that I know he'd have no trouble murdering me while I was "out" (so to speak) means that I trust him a lot more than I should.

The Pardoner's Tale

Happy Birthday

I spat blood and cursed silently. Alex touched his index finger to my lower lip and it came away bloody. He sucked his finger clean and grinned like a maniac.

"Vintage Shifter," he said. "Happy birthday, by the way. You throw a hell of a party."

Emphasis on hell. Alex and I were crouched behind what was left of what had been the door to the stairs that led to our apartment.

Alex and I share a tiny place above a strip club in Baltimore City. It's cramped and cheap, and it's usually not dangerous, but all things change when a vampire enters the equation.

Another vampire, I should say. One who thinks challenging *my* vampire on his home turf is a good idea.

The night started out normal enough, but don't these stories always start out that way? Anyhow, we were in the club, at the bar, "celebrating" my birthday. Sheena (the punk rocker) was on stage providing entertainment for watery-eyed drunks and college students too poor for the more upscale places. And Alex. Me? I was more interested in the brass pocket watch the bartender picked up in Philly.

I was engrossed in the details of the watch when the bartender tapped my arm and used his chin to point at the door.

The stranger wasn't much taller than me, but he was broad. Solid muscle. He had dark hair slicked back and pulled into a ponytail, and doll's eyes.

"Fuck," Alex muttered into his glass. He put the drink down, stood up straight, and squared his shoulders. "You have no business here," he said.

"I have business with you," the new vampire replied. "I've come to challenge you for your territory."

Alex stepped forward. He had almost six inches on this guy. "No. You have no business here."

The stranger's overdeveloped neck muscles made it hard for him to look up at Alex, but he managed. "You really think you can stop me? I'm over a hundred years old. I've got a right to this city. You're just a baby."

Everyone underestimates Alex. He's an idiot. His sire was an idiot. But the thing that a lot of people don't know is that Alex spent the first ten years of his new life in the care of Xyj'Ru, one of the most ruthless demons in the underworld. Alex has skills that have nothing to do with what he is. This wasn't his first challenge, and it wasn't going to be his last.

Alex's nostrils flared. "My grandmother's almost a hundred. Come back when you can impress me."

There was a blur of motion. Never let anyone tell you that vampires aren't fucking *fast*. Suddenly, I was being tossed out of the bar and into the street. I met the sidewalk face-first. Before

I could even clear my head I was airborne again, crashing through the plywood door to the stairs.

There was a wet, snapping sound followed by a pop and a rush of air. Alex climbed through the hole I'd made and knelt next to me. The smear of grey ash on his face was all that remained of the intruder. I spat blood and cursed silently.

Alex touched his index finger to my lower lip. He sucked his finger clean and grinned like a maniac. "Vintage Shifter," he said. "Happy birthday, by the way. You throw a hell of a party."

ABOUT THE AUTHOR

Morgan Ferdinand lives in Baltimore, Maryland with a Canadian, a Welsh terrier, four cats, and a revolving number of tropical fish. There is also knitting.
Find Morgan on Facebook:
https://www.facebook.com/MorganTFerdinand

ABOUT THE ARTIST

Zoe Bentley enjoys naps, tea, fountain pens, repetition, rereading/replaying/rewatching things she's already read/played/watched, and pointing out dogs for no apparent reason. Run if she starts to tell you about a dream she had. You can find her at verilyvexed.tumblr.com.

Made in the USA
Lexington, KY
16 August 2019